THIRTY SHADOW BIRDS

Copyright © 2019 Fereshteh Molavi

Except for the use of short passages for review purposes, no part of this book may be reproduced, in part or in whole, or transmitted in any form or by any means, electronically or mechanically, including photocopying, recording, or any information or storage retrieval system, without prior permission in writing from the publisher or a licence from the Canadian Copyright Collective Agency (Access Copyright).

 Canada Council for the Arts   Conseil des Arts du Canada

We gratefully acknowledge the support of the Canada Council for the Arts and the Ontario Arts Council for our publishing program. We also acknowledge the financial support of the Government of Canada.

Cover design: Val Fullard

Thirty Shadow Birds is a work of fiction. All the characters portrayed in this book are fictitious and any resemblance to persons living or dead, is purely coincidental.

Library and Archives Canada Cataloguing in Publication

Title: Thirty shadow birds : a novel / Fereshteh Molavi.
Names: Molavi, Fereshteh, 1953– author.
Series: Inanna poetry & fiction series.
Description: Series statement: Inanna poetry & fiction series
Identifiers: Canadiana (print) 20190147733 | Canadiana (ebook) 20190147741 | ISBN 9781771336536 (softcover) | ISBN 9781771336543 (epub) | ISBN 9781771336550 (Kindle) | ISBN 9781771336567 (pdf)
Classification: LCC PS8626.O4488 T55 2019 | DDC C813/.6—dc23
Printed and bound in Canada

 MIX Paper from responsible sources FSC® C004071

Inanna Publications and Education Inc.
210 Founders College, York University
4700 Keele Street, Toronto, Ontario, Canada M3J 1P3
Telephone: (416) 736-5356 Fax: (416) 736-5765
Email: inanna.publications@inanna.ca   Website: www.inanna.ca

THIRTY SHADOW BIRDS

a novel by

Fereshteh Molavi

inanna poetry & fiction series

**INANNA PUBLICATIONS AND EDUCATION INC.
TORONTO, CANADA**

I do have a tale, with a bird as a head, with a bird as a tail. Shall I tell it, or shall I not tell it?

Well, tell it!

I do have a tale, with a shadow as a head, with a shadow as a tail. Shall I tell it, or shall I not tell it?

Don't tell it!

I do have a tale…

I say shut up!

Yes, I will shut up; but I do have a shadow bird tale for you, and I do have a shadow bird tale for me…

1.

BUT THIS IS A DREAM!

I cannot see myself. I'm sitting somewhere, I don't know where, staring at a quatrefoil window. I, Yalda the beholder, the invisible, am looking at a Yalda that is visible, right in front of me, here and now, in four shots: Yalda, besotted, in a Montreal pub, staring with eyes wide open at the long forehead of the shadow man who is pressing a napkin to her bleeding right temple; Yalda, injured, in the Montreal emergency room, her eyes closed tight so as not to see the surgeon's hand stitching her head wound; Yalda, offended, in a Toronto office, her eyes fixed on the mouth of Negative Judy, who is spitting words onto her face: "Sorry, Michael didn't include you in the new project"; and Yalda, shocked, in her home looking vacantly at her son wearing a bulletproof vest and duty belt with a baton.

And then I, Yalda the beholder, unable to bear watching, dive through the window to leave behind a broken me, Yalda the tangled, with the echoes of that awful sound: bang, bang, bang.

She feels her body, made of flesh and bones and nerves. With a lump in her throat, dissolving into trickling tears, she opens her eyes to murky light. She still can't determine where she is. Yalda hears him humming in his bass voice:
"*It's raining*
It's pouring

A crazy girl is touring.
Bumped her head,
Went to bed,
And didn't wake up in the morning."

"Ah, I'm at your place again," she whimpers.

"Yeah. Kismet is a bastard! It's our annual meeting, this time in Montreal. A bit late, though," the shadow man replies from behind the canvas curtain that divides his studio. "You had a short nap after those goddamned hours of waiting à *l'urgence*! Make sure you get some rest before you go home."

"Home! I'm not going back to that hell," she laments.

"Okey dokey! Go to the Sheraton Hotel, lady. Or sublet my cave for a month, poor woman. I'm packing my stuff for my tour across Québec."

Having forgotten about her wound, Yalda rolls onto her belly and presses her face against the pillow. The sharp pain makes her groan and roll back onto her side.

"Need a painkiller?" the shadow man asks.

"No! Leave me alone, please!" she sobs.

"Fair enough! I'm going *chez ma blonde*. Your pills and the key are above the fridge. If you happen to disappear, leave the key with the concierge."

She suppresses the urge to blubber by pressing her hand against her mouth. She hears the door creaking.

"If you don't want to end up in a nuthouse, get over this fucking breakdown, girl!" he says, stepping out the door. "It's sink or swim, honey."

As his words and footsteps fade, Yalda stops breathing to savour the complete silence.

"Remember the other time you offered me a story?" the shadowman says, storming back inside and breaking the silence right at the moment Yalda feels a definite urge to resume breathing. "What was it you said? *Shall I tell it, or shall I not tell it?* Well, go ahead and tell it—that can be the rent for my place. Yeah! Spin time and weave your tale, girl!"

Yalda hears him slam the door a second time and finally go away. With the echo of the *bang* resounding in her head, she dashes out of bed and reaches the closed door. She beats her fists against it and bursts into a fit of tears. When her eyes stop tearing up and her wailing comes to an end, she hears her own voice pour out of her mouth; her words are clear: "*Yes. I did have a tale for you ... and I do have a tale for me.... Shall I tell it ... or shall I not tell it? Shut up! Shut up! Shut the fuck up! Yes, I'll shut up, but I do....*"

2.

"AND THEY SEE ONLY THEIR OWN SHADOWS, *or the shadows of one another*...." He breaks off from reading aloud and turns to me with an accusatory glare. His heavy gaze, along with a sudden chilly breeze coming from where he sits, settles on my face. I stop opening the tea thermos, pause, and muster an apologetic smile to prove I'm listening. I know I shouldn't ruin this dubious reunion after so much time has passed. That he is interested in sharing his reading with me is a good sign. It suggests that he is at peace, that his inner skyline is free from ominous clouds. But clouds have no home other than the sky, so they could return at any moment. The reunion is suspect. My goodness! I'm dying to talk to him without any restrictions. Why does he always direct the conversation to what he likes? Nonetheless, I should celebrate this long-awaited moment of companionship. "...*Which the fire throws on the opposite wall of the cave*," he continues. No! That's not a fire behind us. It's a dazzling evening sun, right across from me, on the tangible edge of sky and sea.

BUT THIS IS A DREAM.

To remember it when she is awake, she studies the scene: Guildwood beach, down the bluffs, a fall sunset over the lake, each of them sitting on a rock. He, slouching, immersed in the book; she, back straight and motionless, mesmerized by the sun. It is the perfect picture. But just as she begins to take it in, the sun starts to sink into the dark depths. Gradually, the silent sea swallows not only the sun, but the sky, and finally the dream itself.

And then ripples of pain, sporadic, emerging from the bottom of the sea, creep over her back and gnaw at her sleep. Turning to the other side, she stretches her back to fight the pain. Another defence: she remembers the upcoming visit to her doctor. An eidetic image distracts her: a submissive lakeshore, yielding aggressive ridges, appears for a second and vanishes.

A fugitive visual perception, she thinks.

Yalda senses the light over her closed eyelids. Out there, right behind the white curtains, towards the east, a bit above her sofa bed, another day proclaims itself. Fully awake, she's reluctant to get up. She prays she won't get a call from Negative Julie asking her to take over her morning ESL class. Her internal clock says that it's around seven in the morning. It's not unusual for Negative Julie to wait so late to seek a substitute, as if she gets enormous pleasure from lording her permanent employment over the substitutes; proof of why she deserves the title "Negative." Remaining still, she keeps the thought of a likely call away with an imaginary flyswatter. She had hoped to teach ESL permanently and drop both of her other positions, the AutoCAD teaching gig and the casual project work with the firm, but now her plan is looking iffier than before. Nonetheless, uncertainty is the norm for all the jobs she's tried in North America so far. Isn't that the lot of a newcomer? Or maybe it is a peculiarity of our times. Whatever the hell it is, it sucks!

Now, it's time for her brief pre-rising ritual where she goes over her daily schedule in her mind. Hooked on the habit of perpetually reminding herself of what she's supposed to do, she wonders if she commands her brain, or if her brain commands her. Either way, both she and her brain must prepare to start a new day.

Q: What day is today?
A: Um, Thursday, I guess.
Q: What are your tasks today?
A: At 10:00 a.m., medical appointment, downtown. At 4:00 p.m., class, uptown.
Okay. *Ça suffit!*
Now she is ready to open her eyes and get up.

On the threshold of her room, Yalda pauses to do her brief morning stretches to relieve muscle tension. She holds up her arms to grip the top of the door frame with her fingertips. While she's standing on her tiptoes to stretch her chest forward, in the dull grey light of the room, it seems to her that a stout headless man, squatting and with a big belly, looms on the opposite wall of the living room. Something, a sort of sword, dangles over this massive dark bulge. She feels a cold shiver run down her back and her grip loosens. She places her heels flat on the soft, thick carpet and blinks several times. It's just his backpack and a fishing rod leaning against the wall. Except for the shiny yellow shoulder straps, the bag is all black. On one side is the cooler; on the other the tackle box. Perfect prep! When it comes to camping, she's pretty sure that "procrastination" is not part of his vocabulary. She recalls that, in his clipped, telegraphic style, he announced he would be going camping for a few days. Over the years, she has been forced to get used to this form of conversation.

On her way to the bathroom, Yalda passes the half-closed door to her son's room. She pauses to look at Nader. In his eternal fetal position, his body covered by a blanket, his uncovered face radiates a mild, sweet serenity.

"Asleep in the Deep," she murmurs, recalling the song. "My son is not drowned." She longs to keep looking, but turns away and enters the bathroom.

With her face under the weak stream of the hot water and her eyes closed, Yalda still sees in her mind the face of the young man who sleeps in the only bedroom of her cozy condo in Bayview Village. The bedroom is next to the den where she sleeps, or works, or takes refuge whenever she needs a hole to hide herself in, or to keep the world away. Nevertheless, it seems to her that her son's room is a strange realm not fully open to her. That she sometimes longs to stare at his face when he's asleep is maybe because she hopes to find traces of her sweet baby bird—the delicate face, half-hidden in the pillow or on her bosom, half-visible to her eyes. That still profile, like a sleeping baby bird, made her murmur, "*Oh, mon petit oiseau!*" Nowadays, when she looks at her son, there is no hint of even simple familiarity, let alone that profound, intertwined intimacy they had once shared.

3.

AT THE INTERSECTION OF YONGE AND SHEPPARD, at a red light, Yalda worries about arriving for the appointment on time. It shouldn't take more than an hour to reach the parking lot of St. Michael's College. If nothing happens, she won't be late. But stress is all about ifs, and ifs are the inevitable fruits of an imagination gone wild.

"Should we suppress our imagination in favour of peace of mind?" she argued once with a health counsellor, who became confused and eventually recommended a psychotherapist.

She takes her eyes off the car clock, recalling "Fast Tips to Fight Time Stress." When did she read it? Was it to give her brain a break from her tedious work with AutoCAD or to kill time waiting in a doctor's office? It's not worth bothering her brain about that now. Chinese, Indian, or Tibetan, it was just another American adaptation of an old Eastern method. Ignoring clocks is what one might call "American Fast Stupidity," she thinks, recalling how this expression, a play on American "fast food," made Marc burst into laughter. She can't help but smile, if regretfully. Marc used to tell her that inventors of fast stupidity were not stupid at all, so she shouldn't be unfair. She catches herself before her thoughts continue to linger on Marc. Letting her mind sneak towards thoughts of a colleague, who was once a potential prince charming, is another stupidity, an Eastern type, though—a sign of sentimentalism rooted in her Eastern background and culture. She should keep her mind on a leash to keep it from wandering off. As such, she'd do better to recall the superiority of ignorance over stupidity. After all, who can deny the power of immunity that ignorant people enjoy? Even if the rest of the world can do that, Yalda won't. How could all these drivers in four directions drive, if they didn't ignore the probability of accidents? Even if it would not necessarily save their lives, their ignorance certainly helps them maintain their sanity. And....

An angry driver's honking disrupts her inner debate. She gives him a calm glance in the mirror before turning left on Avenue Road. Well, she admits that whenever she is behind another car taking a left turn, she blames and sometimes even curses that driver for any delay. The driver in front cannot take a risk, though, just to satisfy the person behind him. The golden rule is that our position determines our judgment. What shit! She must stop arguing with herself while she is at the wheel. In fact, it's just as unsafe as talking on a cell phone. Yalda reminds herself to ask the doctor if having a hyperactive mind is somehow related to her sedentary lifestyle. She knows that the doctor tends to relate any "not to her knowledge" physical problems to lifestyle. The interaction between a hard-working mind and a butt addicted to sitting may not even be known to a young general practitioner. Yeah, she'd better give it up and stop thinking.

Avenue Road, from Wilson to Eglinton, seems dull to her. Despite this, such a familiar road relaxes her; the less there is to pay attention to outside, the more she can dive into her thoughts. When her thoughts tend to be gloomy, Yalda knows she has to escape them. She knows some tricks, such as listening to classical music, work well for her. For a moment, she misses NPR Classical—its on-air pledge drives made her less lonely during her frequent solo trips between Montréal and Springfield. They always gave her a sense of belonging to a group of unseen people who loved what she loved. Now is not the right time to listen to her new favourite soundtrack, *The*

Fountain. Without taking her eyes off the road, she turns on the radio. Hearing rap music, she curses Nader for changing the station and tries to bring it back to 99.1 FM by repeatedly pressing the seek button. At last, she recognizes *The Current.* Today, the familiar voice of Anna Maria Tremonti grabs her attention with an interesting hook:

"It's been nearly nineteen years since a gunman walked into the École Polytechnique in Montréal, sat down on a bench for a couple of hours, and then went on a killing rampage. And it's taken nearly nineteen years for his mother to come close to processsing what he did that day...."

On the hump of Avenue Road, where it winds back to a straight continuum before St. Clair, Yalda slows down, pressing the brake to maintain a safe distance from the car in front of her. A sudden doubt about what constitutes a "safe distance" between her and the car in front of her flashes across her mind for a second, then vanishes as the sad voice of the interviewee grabs her full attention:

"It was just 'orrible.... You know..."

Yalda tries to concentrate on the accent. It sounds pleasant to her ears, but the sediment of sorrow in the voice is overwhelming.

"When I heard.... I couldn't believe that...."

She passes Upper Canada College. A woman, maybe as old as that gunman's mother, is walking her puppy along the sidewalk.

"I had the feeling that I was a criminal.... It was 'orrible...."

The woman, well-dressed, has silver hair and a contented, delicate face. Yalda tries to imagine what the old woman in Québec looks like.

"Madame, don't feel guilty about the event.... You know...."

She fails to imagine how she looks. She'll see her picture in the papers or on the computer screen soon, she thinks.

"I didn't raise him to become a killer, you know...."

Yalda notices her palms are wet with sweat. She holds the steering wheel with one hand and dries the palm of the other by rubbing it on her jeans. As the interview continues, the woman repeats the words "you know" over and over, like a refrain. Yalda considers counting them, if only to deviate her attention from the burden of the other words.

"*I was a single mom....*"

Yalda wonders what is behind this statement.

"*He was a narcissist....*"

This is more confusing, she thinks.

"*A little boy, very quiet ... very introverted....*"

Yalda finds her words surprisingly familiar.

"*For me, he was a little boy, you know....*"

Yalda nods, as if the woman is talking to her. When the interviewer asks, "*How much responsibility do you believe a mother has for...*" she turns off the radio and looks out the window at the sombre façade of the Hare Krishna Temple in order to push the interview out of her head for the rest of her trip.

It isn't long before she arrives and all but jumps out of the car, eager to put the drive behind her. When she walks past St. Basil's Church, she pauses for a moment, as if she's forgotten something. She reminds herself that she had heard the signal of the remote control indicating she'd locked the car doors. She gazes at her favourite church in the city, with its brick façade and aquamarine roof, which always makes her think of those lovely bricks and tiles of her lost past. This time, for no reason, it reminds her of the woman on the radio, a mother like her, a woman far away from her, but not a stranger anymore.

"Pardon, Madame. This is not a good time," Yalda whispers in embarrassment, and rushes towards the clinic.

While checking in, Yalda glances at the clock. She's on time; she can relax. She looks around. The waiting room is very small and includes a partitioned office for the secretary, with several rooms around it. It's not only the old building and furniture, but also the lack of any kind of harmony that announces how modest the office's budget is. Oddly, this is another reason to feel comfortable. She'd be skeptical in a luxurious doctor's office, assuming that it was the patients who were paying for it. She's against private health care, but she's not sure whether she would remain a supporter of the public health system if she had more money. Yet, as a born admirer of beauty, she hungers to find harmony in any space, and so its absence here is mildly disquieting.

Taking a seat, she ponders the health system's flaws. It's taken about six months for her to find a family physician after moving to her new condo. She's been picky about choosing a doctor, she has to admit. The reason for this is that she believes there should be trust from the first visit. A female colleague eventually recommended this clinic, telling Yalda that the clinic had been a pioneer in women's healthcare.

A baby's cry, coming out of the half-open door of the corner room next to the entrance, pierces her ears. She wishes there was a mute button—she has to concentrate. While the baby gasps for breath in between screams, she can hear the soft anxious voice of a young mother plying the nurse with questions. She feels some sympathy for the mother. She hardly remembers Nader ever screaming even though he was more or less always sick before he started school—not a boisterous baby at all. He was quite calm in the doctor's office, to the point that once she suspected the nurse had not really given him a vaccine shot. When the mother comes out of the room, the baby still screaming, Yalda wonders if, in twenty years, she will be able to admit how annoying her baby was.

The doctor is a young pregnant blonde in a denim trapeze dress that is a bit tight for her at the top. She looks like a peasant woman with her red cheeks, cheerful face, and stout torso. While Yalda tells about her back pain, the doctor's smile crinkles the skin around her eyes. She doesn't look so young as to be having her first baby. When the doctor advises her to change her lifestyle, Yalda is annoyed. It's all about "how" not "why," she thinks. The doctor moves her chair a bit to use the small desk in the corner to write a prescription. Yalda looks at the doctor's belly to gauge how many months pregnant she is.

"I can take care of you only for a few months. Is that okay with you?" the doctor asks, without taking her eyes from the prescription.

"Well, you'll have a replacement. Won't you?"

The doctor nods. "I'll be on leave for six months," she says.

"Is it your first time? Your first baby?"

The doctor takes her eyes off the paper. "Oh, no, he's going to be my fourth," she says smiling.

Yalda wonders whether or not she should show her astonishment. The doctor makes it easy for her by turning her eyes back to the paper.

"How brave you are!" Yalda says, and her mind goes back to the Montréal mom she'd heard interviewed on the radio.

4.

THE OCTOBER DAY IS GREY AND UNINSPIRING, and Yalda decides not to hang around downtown. She looks at her watch to see how many hours she has before she has to go to the college. To kill time, she opens the door of Timothy's coffee shop at the corner of Bay and Charles. It is quiet as usual, and thankfully her favourite spot is free. A bit depressing, but good for daydreaming, she thinks as she orders her coffee. Sitting on the club chair, she imagines it in a more modern style with a different pattern and colour. She curses this habit of picturing furniture looking different, once so pleasant and now so troublesome. She turns her head towards the window to watch passersby, her gaze blank.

Yalda remembers her last night's dream, realizing that it was not exotic, uncommon, or even remarkable; it was just tasty enough to be chewed over. It was not a genuine dream by any means, only a reproduction of something that had happened in waking life two years ago. When was it? The first semester of Nader's freshman year, she recalls. Both of them were excited, but in different ways. They were also both pretending that nothing had changed. But after a long period of single-parenting an aloof, indifferent teen, she noticed her son expressing a mild interest in his chosen field: philosophy. Not to make waves, Yalda gave up grumbling over his choice. She'd learned over the years that Nader would go deaf if there was a hint of advice in her words, let alone a lecture.

Then, out of the blue, a small miraculous thing happened on a Friday evening. Right after coming home, Nader proposed going to the beach on Saturday afternoon, no matter what the weather was like. So they went to Guildwood, down the bluffs, to watch the fall sunset over the lake. Each of them sitting on a rock, Nader read aloud some lines from Plato with obvious fascination, and she listened to his voice with satisfaction. Then there was silence again. With all her body and soul, she channelled the feeling of the sunset ahead of her; she sensed the generous vastness of the earth; and she sipped the mild sweetness of simple happiness.

AND IT WAS NOT A DREAM.

Gradually, the silent sea swallowed not only the sun, but the sky itself.

5.

NO, SHE DIDN'T SEE IT. NOT IN THE MORNING when she got out of the car, and not a while ago when she got back into it. It's only now, a second after turning onto Bay and passing the parking lot, that Yalda sees the dark grey steel and glass presentation gallery, signalling that one more condo tower will soon pop out of the earth. It's not surprising that she doesn't recall any news about it; her serving of daily media has been reduced to nil. She can't help but notice the hard humps on the city skyline, reminding her of a Stegosaurus under the burden of its bony plates. That a tower or two will make St. Basil's look dull is something that she cannot do anything about, and so she is sad that they will dwarf her beloved aquamarine tower.

Before turning onto Yonge, she reaches her hand into the small plastic bag of fruit she usually carries on her teaching days. She likes to eat an apple or peach or nectarine while driving on Yonge to her evening class. It gives her some energy before the class and makes the long trip seem shorter. It's more than that, though. Munching on the fruit as she drives toward Yonge and Lawrence always enhances her pleasure as she sneaks glances at the store windows on both sides of the street. Sometimes she is tempted to take the Don Valley Parkway, not because she prefers a fast trip, but simply because the road runs through a green valley. However, the busy freeway often doesn't allow her to enjoy the scenery. Not to mention that slender Yonge Street, with its multitude of boutiques, appeals to her European sensibilities.

At the red light on Davisville, Yalda, an apple core between her teeth, enjoys the amusing variation of faces and figures, shapes, and colours passing at the pedestrian crossing. In the middle of the human wave moving in front of her eyes, she detects something familiar—an elephantine head on top of a mouse-like body, with panda eyes and jet-black hair, gelled upright like a hoopoe's crest.

"Dr. Ahmaqi!" Yalda says under her breath, and the apple core falls to the floor.

She bends to grab the core and, straightening her back, bangs her temple on the edge of the sun visor.

"Okay! I got punished by the invisible hand of heaven," she mumbles. She remembers that the man's name is Dr. Ahmadi, which means "admirable"; not Ahmaqi, which means "idiot."

"He's a genius; he's not stupid," she says, this time aloud, resentful.

From the first moment of her first visit with him, Yalda felt an urge to call him Ahmaqi instead of Ahmadi. Was this an overt bias, the wisdom of first impressions, or just for the pun? Clearly, she never called him by that name outright, even when they quarrelled. On the morning of her fourth day at work, when she was sent to the freezer to get something, she repeated that name four times under her breath, shivering and wiping tears off her frozen cheeks. On the afternoon of the fourth day, she learned that Mrs. Ahmadi, his wife, had fired her—the first job Yalda had found after four months of hunting for work. Yalda was glad she hadn't missed the opportunity to take revenge on Mrs. Ahmadi's husband earlier that day by calling him by the name that suited him most.

Somebody behind her honks his horn. She looks into the rear-view mirror, steps on the gas, and waves an apology. She allows herself to think about the man who rose above the human current for a minute and then disappeared, like scum on running water. But scum, like scars, never go away. One of her college students, an architect back home and a kitchen helper in Toronto, said this to her once. As the student described her humiliating working conditions, she tried to hide her scarred hands under her armpits; the pain was obvious in her broken voice.

Yalda looks at her own hands resting on the steering wheel. No scars; no traces. Not on the skin; not on the surface. Down there, beneath the skin, maybe in the folds and grooves of her brain's grey matter, she hides all the scars, all the scum.

It was not Dr. Ahmadi's disproportionate body or the oddity of his facial features that gave Yalda a bad impression of him. It was his attitude. It swelled like a balloon in the course of the four days she worked for the Ahmadis in their bakery/café franchise, and eventually burst when, after one final insult about her many "failures," her anger and humiliation reached a boiling point, and she broke down in tears.

Missing a yellow light, Yalda slams on the brakes to stop at the red. Another failure, she thinks.

The last straw was when he had pointed out her inability to toast a bagel for a condescending customer. "No wonder Ahmadi deserves to be called Ahmaqi," she chides aloud as she recalls the incident.

She tries to forget the way he looked at her, not only during that thorny discussion, but also when he spied on her to make sure she was doing her job.

Yalda notices a fluffy chocolate-coloured puppy looking at her through the window of a flashy car. A smile comes to her lips, but quickly vanishes when the dog begins to bark aggressively. Her mind goes back to the man who could be demoted from "admirable" to "idiot" just by a simple change of "d" to "q."

Dr. Ahmadi, who used to be a university professor in Iran, was unhappy with his wife's decision to hire her because he considered Yalda overqualified. When Mrs. Ahmadi introduced her, and mentioned Yalda had been an architect, a smug grin appeared on his face. From day one, he looked down on her. He wanted it to be clear that she was no more than a "help unwanted" newcomer with no "Can Exp": not quick enough to comprehend the customers' mumbled orders; not savvy enough to know how to make and serve breakfast, salad, soup, and sandwiches; not smart enough to interact with customers.

"Go to hell, Dr. *Ahmaqi*. You made me lose my confidence," Yalda mutters. Yet she has to admit that this is not the root of her anger.

The light turns green. It's time, perhaps, Yalda thinks, to look beneath the surface. What vexed her was that he was right. Despite what she claimed, she had zero talent as a waitress. More than that, she was reluctant to cater to stomachs, either hers or those of others—the only exception was her Little Bird's stomach.

Other girls, and even the chef, that bulky Slav with sweat flowing off his red chubby face, knew that Mrs. Ahmadi was the real boss, and they always called her Madame. In reply to the nonstop orders of her husband, though, they would say, "Yes, boss! No, boss! Okay, boss!" The Ethiopian girl, who was supposed to train Yalda, used to whisper, "He's a bossy boss," and they would both titter.

Yalda recalls that she had been taken aback when Mrs. Ahmadi had first introduced her to her husband. She had referred to him as her "full partner," rather than her "better half," and considering the tacky, dollar store tie that dangled around his neck, Yalda couldn't blame her. She had been unable to hide her surprise and Mrs. Ahmadi had noticed. After the meeting, which was an informal interview, she had shrugged to shake the guilt from her shoulders, reminding herself that beauty is in the eye of the beholder.

They were an unusual pair. Mrs. Ahmadi was tall, slim, stylish, with honey brown eyes, delicate hands, and well-manicured nails. Yalda had been inclined to imagine that business people were snooty or boring, but Mrs. Ahmadi seemed nice. Yalda wondered how she kept her hands so beautiful. During their interview, Mrs. Ahmadi had been doubtful about hiring Yalda; she had been concerned that the position did not suit her. But Yalda had been tenacious. A mutual friend, who'd also been an architect back home and had rented a room in her house to Yalda, had told them about each other. Yalda explained that as a newcomer, a single mom, and a woman without any support or savings, she needed the job to survive. She implored them to kindly ignore her background as an architect. It had been four months since she and Nader had landed in Toronto, and, despite all her efforts, she hadn't succeeded in finding a job. Mrs. Ahmadi wondered if she'd tried French tutoring. Yalda told her it had been her first idea, but that the school, claiming a false bankruptcy, wouldn't pay her in full. Noticing the sympathy in Mrs. Ahmadi's eyes, Yalda smiled and told her she hadn't expected Canada to roll out a red carpet for her when she decided to emigrate. The vertical frown line between Mrs. Ahmadi's eyebrows got darker and the fine wrinkles around the corner of her mouth deepened.

"Besides, our mutual friend does not work as an architect after all this time, and neither do you," Yalda let slip, later regretting her words.

"Not a convincing comparison, you know," Mrs. Ahmadi replied with a vague smile and hesitant tone. "Our friend preferred to make money as a realtor. And me, well, you may know that I married a wealthy man, a university professor, oddly enough, who also happened to own restaurants and discos. But then...."

Mrs. Ahmadi's story reminded Yalda of *All The Shah's Men*, a book she'd recently read. People just like the Ahmadis lose their king, and all their puffy daydreams go with him, she thinks. Pretending to listen, Yalda could imagine Mrs. Ahmadi's story. *Yes, you left all your belongings and fled abroad in the hope of returning soon. Alas!*

When Mrs. Ahmadi's narrative reached a certain point, Yalda began to listen.

"...I didn't want to raise my twins in Texas, you know. We moved to Canada for them. My husband couldn't get an academic position in the United States or in Canada, even with a Ph.D. from Britain. Obviously, I couldn't work as an architect as a graduate of the University of Tehran with little work experience. We decided to start up a small business. And you know, the fast-food business is a safe business."

Yalda was not brave enough to reveal her work experience in a chelow-kabab restaurant in Saint-Étienne to a prospective boss who was also a fellow countrywoman, so she just insisted that she would not mind a menial job.

"It's not that easy to be a simple labourer, you know," Mrs. Ahmadi insisted.

"I'll do my best to learn how to do the job. As a single mom, I am familiar with making sandwiches," Yalda said with a grin.

"I'm concerned about whether others will accept you." Mrs. Ahmadi put her cards on the table. "Nevertheless, you can try it for a few days and we'll see if it works for you and for us."

As it turned out, it didn't. When she handed the bagel and cream cheese to her first customer—a white-faced, blue-eyed guy in a well-tailored suit—she noticed a frown between his eyebrows. He didn't say anything, though. During the break, her Ethiopian colleague mentioned that the gentleman—she didn't call all male customers gentlemen—didn't like his bagel to be too crunchy. The customer hadn't told her about his preference. She resisted the urge to defend herself; instead, she swallowed what felt like too much saliva in her mouth.

Later, she got another sign. The boss, not the real boss but the bossy boss, wanted to see her on her lunch break. When she went to his office, she was prepared to accept the blame and apologize. But not only did he lecture her about customer service, he also yelled at and threatened her. He definitely crossed the line.

Recalling the meeting, Yalda questions whether the volume of his voice was high enough to be called yelling. His tone had been accusatory, decisive, and harsh. Most likely, it was his look that had been so offensive to her. While listening to him, she had felt all the pressure and stress of the four-day learning process. She had had to learn so much in so little time: the names of different breads, pastries, cheeses, drinks, soups, salads, sauces, etc., the types of sandwiches, the ways of wrapping, the sorts of smiles she could practise on customers, and on and on. The worst was the moment just before a customer ordered—what if she couldn't understand what they meant? For three nights, she'd suffered from the same nightmare: one by one the customers came to her, stood in front of her, fixed their eyes on her, opened their mouths, and showed her all their speech organs—teeth, tongue, alveolar ridge, hard palate, velum, uvula, and glottis—without uttering a word, or even producing a sound. Dr. Ahmadi's head floated above them. A hoopoe's fan-like crest, sitting on top of his head like a crown, opened and closed nonstop while his mouth spewed out words, sounds, and saliva.

When she reaches the campus parking lot, she finds it hard to shake off thoughts of her first boss. She looks at her watch. She has time to put Dr. Ahmadi out of her mind and refocus on the task at hand. Before doing that, though, she articulates out loud what was on the tip of her tongue back then: "Boss, I may be a failure, but you're Dr. Ahmaqi!"

6.

HER FINGER HOVERS ABOVE THE "G" BUTTON. She hesitates to press it, though. Is she looking forward to any letter? No. What will she find in the mailbox other than flyers and bills? She's not expecting anything, so there's no reason to stop at the ground floor and check. Yalda's finger jumps up to "7."

The lock on her apartment door is finicky, and Yalda pauses outside for a few moments, trying to turn the key. Nobody rushes to open the door. She bites her lower lip, trying to remember the trick. When the door finally opens, she lingers at the threshold, wondering where Nader is. Her eyes take in the living room and the small galley kitchen. "Not bad at all," she says with shallow conviction followed by forced deep breathing.

Once in a while she needs a break, time to get her mind off her son, her dearest attachment, and the rest of the world. But first, she has to face the mountain of dirty dishes that Nader has left in the sink and on the counters. The living room doesn't look so bad. And his room? Well, it can be made invisible with a closed door.

Having done the chores, she feels like a drink. She doesn't buy alcohol often, so all she can find are a few Molsons, Nader's favourite, in the fridge. She puts a glass of beer on the side table next to the ceramic bowl of nuts and dried berries, and a porcelain plate filled with fresh fruit. Pushing her rocking chair towards the table, Yalda resists the idea of making it a festive feast by adding a plate of sweets. She wants to sit on her throne like the Queen of Sheba daydreaming about a contemporary Solomon with wealth and wisdom, but the red flashing light of the answering machine distracts her.

"One more chore left," she grumbles, pressing the button.

There are two messages: one from Julie, the other from Judy; both negative versions of heroines from her teenage years—Julie Andrews from *The Sound of Music* and Judy Abbott, the protagonist of *Daddy-Long-Legs*. While Negative Julie asks her to supply-teach, Negative Judy, the secretary of the architecture firm, informs Yalda in her steely voice that the project has been put on hold.

It's not quite a *memento mori,* Yalda thinks to herself, but it's certainly a hint that you're in the downturn of the "hire-fire" cycle. This doesn't stop her from kicking off her solitary feast. She reclines in her chair, raises her glass, and says *à ta santé* to her shadow on the wall. Later on, Yalda may dance with her shadow, if she feels the warmth of alcohol in her veins. Right now, she has to process the data she has received.

Yalda picks up a handful of dried mulberries. When she savours the familiar sweetness, redolent of flashes from her childhood, she feels her scattered thoughts fall into place. It's true that Canada has more opportunities than Europe for architects. And, she isn't the type to leave her chosen field in order to make money. She's completely lost touch with her ex-roommate, now a realtor in T.O., shovelling money into her bank account. And thank goodness she didn't marry her ex-classmate, Fari, who became a rug seller in Rome in order to have a glimpse of luxury.

That the project has been postponed is a sign. It means the recession, like an octopus, has been reaching out with one of its legs to touch the robes of the Emirates' sheikhs. She heard the buzz about the closing of the office in Dubai a while ago, but nobody had seemed worried about the firm's future. Everybody thought the sole proprietor knew how to get through hard times. Michael, the principal in charge of the team Yalda worked with, cut staff turnover to prove he was more cautious than the big boss.

Michael, that WASP, cannot ruin her evening, though. With an egg in the ESL basket, and another in the AutoCAD basket, Yalda can sip her beer so as to enjoy every drop of it. Imagining Michael, the beer guzzler, sitting in front of her on the sofa, she puts an almond in her mouth and grins. "*Mais oui!* It's true that the third egg, in fact the first egg, the one that looked the biggest and the brightest, is now in your hands, dear Michael," she says with her softest voice. "Nonetheless, since I'm enjoying my drink, *frankly, my dear, I don't give a damn*," she says, imitating Clark Gable.

Later, when she spits the white foam of toothpaste into the sink and rinses her mouth, she thinks that despite her dull day, she's had a nice evening: drink, fruit, snacks, music, a good book, and solitude. On her way to her bedroom, she mentally runs through the list of materials she needs for Julie's class, making sure that they're in her bag. Before she closes her bedroom door, she takes one final look around to make sure that the stove is off and the front door is locked—it's important for her to confirm that everything is in order; otherwise she will obsess over it after she lies down.

"But my pillow is missing again," she mumbles.

For a moment, Yalda's heart beats for her son. That he has kept this habit from childhood up to now is a sweet secret. When he was a baby, it had been difficult to wean him, and she succeeded in doing so only when she made her breasts peppery. Then her happy baby became a horrible sleeper. Nothing she tried worked until she found out that, afraid to touch her breasts anymore, he had replaced them with her pillow. Soon, he could only sleep with her pillow, and it began to make the trip between her bed and his every night. At first, it didn't seem to be a troublesome issue. After a while, though, it turned out that Yalda, as well, could not sleep without her own pillow. Even though she tried to let go of this obsession with belongings, she failed and eventually gave up. When Nader was a child, she always waited her turn: when he fell into a deep sleep, she slipped into his room and took back the pillow from his loosened grip. Years later, when he became a tough teenage boy, he didn't ask her for the pillow anymore, but after she got up he would wander into her bedroom like a sleepwalker and take it back to bed with him.

Yalda goes to Nader's room to pick up the pillow. When she opens the door, she tries to avert her eyes from the mess. She can't help seeing it, though: heaps of mingled stuff—clothes, clean and dirty, papers, books, assignments from high school and university, discs, old and new—on top of the overstuffed desk or chair or dresser or bed, all over the floor, and even hanging on the always open door of the closet. She holds her breath so as to not notice the smelly stray socks strewn across everywhere. Tomorrow, after work, she must clean up a bit, as much as she can without making him crazy.

Yalda walks towards the bed. Before she reaches the pillow sitting on the tumbled, crumpled quilt, her bare feet slide over some papers. She stumbles and smacks her knee against the corner of the desk.

"Damn it!" She kneels to pick up the paper. It's an open envelope with a folded form sticking out of it. She can read the bold title at the top of the page. It's an application form, with Nader's name in the first box. Her mind reeling, she refuses to believe what her eyes have just read. As the shock fades, her head begins to spin. She can feel her body's rivers and brooks, bright and dark, turning to stone, and whatever flows and moves under her skin, turning to lead.

7.

IT'S HARD NOT TO COLLAPSE. NOT TO CRY. *Not to put this damned head on the desk and make a protective fort with my arms to detach my eyes and mind from my surroundings, as I used to do when I was a student.* And as my poor student, Asuntha, does before her "folly." Asuntha's madness is mild, though. Mine is not going to be mellow at all. This is what the jinn wanted me to understand last night. Damn it! After all, the jinn knows me well. She is my "hamzad"—we were born on the same day at the exact same time, I in this nasty world and she in the world of jinns. So, she appeared last night after I'd found the papers. The jinn showed me a tiny spot in her unfolded fist and pointed at her head silently and viciously, as if predicting I would soon become insane. I denied it. Although I was shocked to discover my son's secret, I was not going crazy. The shock had felt like a loud bang *in my head, and it left me with nothing but a question mark.*

In the morning, when I got up, there was *no sign of the jinn and her ominous gesture.* Instead, I saw a patch of sunlight, evidence of a new day, on my shady wall. It would keep the jinn away from me. I know that my hamzad, unlike me, doesn't like sunlight at all. But, even so, I thought she might come back, because even in the morning light, I felt a question mark, this time a giant one, hovering over my head.

Suddenly a feeling of uneasiness comes upon me. I sense that the jinn is screaming somewhere. I can't actually hear her, but

I know how bolshie and pushy and difficult my hamzad is. I'm just as stubborn as she is, though. I'm going to prove to her here and now that I have no room for her. I'm going to call up all my willpower to complete a half day's work. The rest of the day will be mine to cut and run, to howl like a wounded lonely wolf, and then ... then to lie down in my den like a dead body relieved of all its senses.

Other than Asuntha, disconnected, face down under the black tent of her long, thick hair, nobody is in the classroom. Yalda looks at the clock. Ten more minutes of break remaining. It's too cold to go out for a breath of fresh air. She could venture down to the first floor for coffee, but its flavour is mingled with the odd smell of a South Asian supermarket, and it doesn't appeal to her. She'd rather stay in the small, windowless classroom and doodle on scrap paper to take her mind off disturbing thoughts. In the corridor, students often stop by to socialize with their "non-blonde Canadian" teacher. The building, one of the many newly constructed retail buildings in Mississauga, has—besides soon-to-be-opened stores—some doctors' offices and two ESL classrooms: one is for a literacy class and the other for a multi-level class. Students, mostly female, like to chat in small groups, while men, old or young, prefer to stay away from these circles. Yalda enjoys joining the women or just watching them, and exchanging a few words with her male students during the break. This makes them happy, for Julie has no time for them outside the class, either because she always arrives late or is busy on her cellphone at the break. According to Nandita, another student, she always leaves class at five o'clock on the dot.

Yalda tries to sketch a picture of Nandita in a sitting pose. Nandita acted as the monitor of the class on Yalda's first day covering for Julie, and she really proved herself. As soon as Yalda stepped into the classroom on her first day, she heard a ringing voice: "Good morning, new teacher!" It was a brown woman in a sari casting her dark eyes around and commanding the class. Following their conductor, the students chanted in unison, "Good morning, new teacher!" Yalda couldn't help chuckling at this ESL chorus of broken English. As she got to know her better, Yalda began to understand that Nandita was always the person in charge, wherever she went. She even had a special seat in the middle of the second row, where she could keep an eye on the students in the front and in the back.

Later, Nandita started to take any opportunity, inside and outside the classroom, to advise, complain, report to, and open her heart to Yalda, who was "the best teacher" and "the best listener" she had ever met in Canada. Perhaps this was why Nandita had offered her honourary assistantship. She was very qualified for the role. After all, she had been the principal of a large girls' high school in Bombay; her English was pretty good, far better than any other student in the class; and she could even read their minds, speak on their behalf, help them do their homework, and most importantly, correct them.

This last task soon became problematic. Nandita could not keep her mouth shut when she heard someone say something wrong. The English part of her brain had zero tolerance for any detectable errors. On the other hand, her heart directed her to be of help to anybody in the class, including Abdul Qader, the grumpiest old man Nandita had ever met in Canada.

Yalda chooses a space on her paper, away from Nandita's figure, to draw Abdul Qader giving her a dirty look. He is hardly older than Nandita, who calls herself a "mature woman." Both, however, look older than their real age. Abdul Qader is as introverted as Nandita is outgoing. He is self-conscious about his accent, and he is very aware of his errors, which makes him timid. To break the ice, sometimes Nandita takes it upon herself to discuss everything she knows about Egypt: the pyramids, the Great Sphinx of Giza, even Om Kalthoum and Omar Sharif. Nothing is wrong with this, even though he is from Egypt and Nandita is not. Sometimes Abdul Qader joins in, but he quickly becomes quiet if she interrupts or corrects him too many times.The first time Nandita interjects, Abdul Qader frowns and blushes; the second time, he shakes his head restlessly; and the third time, his face becomes swollen and purple, and he gives Nandita the dirtiest look on earth, as he flicks his mouth with curled fingers. When this happens, Nandita, apologizing, rushes out of the classroom and heads to the washroom to splash cool water over her face and close her eyes. She imagines herself in a prayer alcove, begging her gods to negotiate with Allah so that Abdul Qader does not have a heart attack because of her good will.

Yalda's right hand, holding a blunt pencil, slides over the paper towards her sketch of Nandita. She is wondering what to add to it when she sees Nandita enter the classroom with a smile on her face, carrying a package of her half-moon-shaped *karanji* pastries wrapped in delicate burgundy paper. Yalda flips over her sheet of paper.

"Teacher, help yourself!" Nandita says, nodding her head and stretching out her hand.

Yalda knows she can't avoid trying Nandita's homemade date and fig *karanjis*, and she accepts one so that Nandita can carry on with her mission. Whenever Asuntha has one of her episodes, Nandita tells the class that the demon has come back to torment Asuntha. She says, "It's good to put some sweet stuff into Asuntha's body." Heavenly date and fig *karanji* is a present that no one could resist, including Sri Lankan demons.

Asuntha's demon doesn't show any interest in Nandita's exquisite homemade pastries today. The more Nandita pats Asuntha on the shoulder, whispering incantations in Hindi, the less Asuntha reacts. Asuntha often draws pictures of her demon to keep herself busy during class. Today, Yalda tries her hand at drawing a demon as well, but it doesn't look anything like Asuntha's. Asuntha's demon, besieged by a crabbed English alphabet, looks funny. Yalda, on the other hand, draws a more formidable demon, like the one who infiltrated a corner of

Asuntha's brain and took up residence there. This happened long before Asuntha's brother could sponsor her and bring her to Canada. According to Nandita's detective work, the demon, who had been meandering around Asuntha's village, ran into the pretty little girl after she was thrown onto the porch by her stepmother, who was sick of her nonstop crying. The demon saved the pretty little girl's life and got a cozy dwelling in return.

"Teacher, you are having aspirin, no?" Nandita asks.

Yalda shakes her head and casts a sideways glance at the clock. "Nandita, please call the students to come back to class."

"Mrs. Teacher. First, Asuntha, second, the class," she replies decisively, shaking her head. Nandita adds "Mrs." to teacher so that Yalda will understand that her statement is meant as a lesson.

"Goodness, where am I?" Yalda asks. "In an ESL class with students, all wise and ... all visible minorities," she murmurs quietly to herself.

Yalda glances towards the cork bulletin board, noticing a colour photo that has been pinned there. It shows students gathered around Julie and Elizabeth, the program coordinator. Elizabeth, one of the dominant majority, is singled out among the visible minorities, Julie, a brown woman from Australia, and her brown-skinned Asian students. While Elizabeth's smile is as pale as her skin, the students' grins all show their teeth. Their smiles are as shiny as their dark skin.

Yalda's thoughts are interrupted when she senses a silent presence nearby. She turns her head and sees Rima tiptoeing into the room, looking upset. Yalda recalls that, according to Nandita, Rima's world revolves around her teenaged son, a reminder of her beloved husband.

"Are you okay, Rima?" Yalda asks her, smiling.

Rima stops and casts her eyes down to avoid eye contact.

"Is something wrong with your son, Rima?" Yalda asks.

"He don't come home, teacher," Rima whispers.

"Again? Did he go to his uncle's?" Yalda asks, disliking

her investigative tone. A feeble "sorry" slips out of her half-closed mouth, in response to either her sense of guilt or Rima's nodding. To change the subject, she says, "Could you call the other students back to class, Rima?"

Rima turns back to the corridor. She's nothing like Nandita, Yalda says to herself. Not a brooder or shy, she's a quiet woman with an enigmatic story. So far it has been revealed partly by Nandita's indefatigable journalistic efforts and partly by Rima herself, in fits and starts. Born into a Christian Syrian family, she fell in love with a refugee, a Shia survivor of the Sabra and Shatila massacre. When her family found out about the relationship, they threatened her and her lover, and the two of them escaped to Lebanon. She gave birth to a son on the same day that her husband was killed by a Phalangist militiaman. Then she fled again, this time as a UN refugee, from her controlling brother-in-law, a fundamentalist Shia. Supposedly, destiny moves ahead of us; Rima is a case in point. Now the brother-in-law has come to Toronto himself, and she cannot prevent her son from seeing his only uncle, who's obsessed with his brother's murder.

Yalda feels a shiver run down her back as she stands up, struggling to put on a happy face in front of the class.

8.

LOOKING AROUND FOR A SEAT, Yalda finds that her favourite hideout is free. She drags her tired feet across the pub and lands on the corner leather sofa, half-hidden behind a pillar. The furthest and dimmest spot of a basement pub might be the first choice of couples looking for a "love" seat, but luckily there are no customers at this time of day other than Yalda and a man with a shaved head who is slumped over the counter at the other end.

The waiter, a young punk guy with his hair styled in soft spikes, comes to her. Without looking at the menu, she asks for a martini. She's not going to get drunk, she thinks, but she should lift her spirits. A drink and some alone time are what she needs to get ready for what is coming her way tonight. But what if the jinn, her *hamzad*, comes to her here and now?

No. The jinn didn't appear in broad daylight either on the bloody day of her brother's murder in the December of '91, or on the bloody day of her boyfriend's execution in May of '80. After each of those loud *bangs*, when she felt like her head was about to explode, her *hamzad* had emerged only during the night.

This may prove that her poor mother, Maman Ashi, was not altogether wrong when she boasted about her expertise in jinn studies. Maman Ashi believed that jinns don't like to visit in the daytime. She also asserted that one can make a jinn withdraw by uttering the name of God in Arabic. Because Yalda was a non-believer, her jinn supposedly had no fear of her evoking the name of Allah, a practice that is known as *bismallah*. And maybe her jinn is mature enough to know that daytime is not the right time to reveal insanity.

Bang! Bang! Bang!

The sound in her head warns her that what occurred last night triggered a tremendous anxiety and fear of unpredictable threats. Suddenly, Yalda sees the jinn peeping out from behind the pillar and grinning at her. The waiter, bringing her order, blocks her view of the jinn for a minute. She welcomes his interruption, using the time to figure out how to treat her unpunctual *hamzad*. When the waiter leaves, she looks at the jinn and points to her watch. The jinn, still chuckling, opens her mouth four times to insist that this new loud *bang* is going to occur. The jinn's gestures, which remind her of Bollywood dance moves, get on her nerves. She keeps pointing to her watch until the jinn gets the message, shakes her head, and disappears without producing any smoke—more evidence that her *hamzad* has nothing to do with the jinns known to Maman Ashi.

Yalda breathes a sigh of relief and sips her drink. The man with the shaved head shifts on his bar stool but doesn't turn around. As long as his back is to her, she can amuse herself by guessing what he looks like. She is only here is to kill time. After her class in Mississauga, she drove home, parked in the basement garage, took the southbound subway downtown and, after a long walk, ended up here.

Distraction for procrastination. Alcohol for dissolution. Betrayal for betrayal. The first two were part of her plan, and the third was at the back of her mind. Jostled while wandering down Yonge Street's busy sidewalk, she stopped for a second to regain her balance. For some reason, she dug her cell phone out of her purse and browsed the list, as if looking for someone to call for help. She pressed the button when it reached Jimmy's number. *Beep! Beep! Beep!* Fixing her eyes on the phone, she felt a flush of shame and a burning sensation in her palm. She turned off the phone and threw it back into the purse. A gust of wind, slapping her face and stinging her skin, let the hot tears run down her cold cheeks.

The shame didn't come up from a single place. She's ashamed that she had thought about a lecherous guy like Jimmy even though she had no desire for him, and that she had no male friend, with or without benefits, to turn to in tough times. She's also ashamed of her plan to seek revenge on Nader, her Little Bird, by sleeping with an unwanted man. It was so stupid—Nader wouldn't give a damn about what she did or how she felt.

Yalda empties her glass in one gulp and turns her eyes towards the bar to get the waiter's attention. She notices the broad shoulders of the guy with the shaved head, who looks like he's sitting on nails. Neither his oval head reflecting the red lamplight nor his thick biceps protruding from his short-sleeved black T-shirt are appealing. She wonders how she found big-chested men attractive when she was a teenager. Her only brother, Dadash Yunes, was tall and slim. With his dark, thick hair, combed to the left, he looked handsome when he was young. But, for one reason or another, he was never idolized by his younger sister. And when Yalda met her first boyfriend, the world changed. She would later name her son after him. Nader, the one who she used to call *"Nader-am"* (my Nader), changed her perspective. She never found big-chested men attractive again.

Enjoying her second martini, Yalda closes her eyes, imagining a companion. An instant image of a dark, thick-haired man appears behind her closed eyelids. It is not an image of Yunes, from a time when he was so dear to her that he was called Dadashi. She bites her lower lip and opens her eyes. If the image had lasted a little bit longer, she could have said, "Hello dark-haired man!" It was a humorous greeting, one she used to use when she dated Daniel Dunn, the marketing manager of the firm. She liked his dark hair that had resisted turning grey.

Her vibrating cell phone pushes Dan away. Immediately, she begins to worry about her son, Nader. "Stupid woman," she grumbles while she picks up the phone. Nader never ever calls her when he's in town, let alone when he's out camping. She sees Jimmy's number and feels disgusted with herself. It took a lot of effort for her to make him understand that she wouldn't be the right partner for a thirty-year-old guy with a wolfish appetite for sex. And now she had opened up the situation again with her silly, impulsive call!

Trying to think of an excuse for calling Jimmy makes Yalda feel dizzy. She gives up and focuses on the soft chitchat of a cuddling couple to her left. She's getting drunk, she confesses. It's not time to go home, though. The jinn, never predictable, will be waiting to point out that her son has treated her like crap. As if she was not intelligent enough to get it last night. "Idiot jinn! What the hell are you going to tell me?" she says under her breath. The couple notices her. The man looks about the same age as Dan, but the girl doesn't look much older than a teenager. He could have been Dan, she says to herself. The girl, giggling, slides her fingers through his hair and lets them slip down to the lines of his forehead. Maybe this guy, like Dan, has four grown-up daughters and a lovely wife sharing not only her bank account but also her free time with him. Maybe he, like Dan, is not willing to put his marriage at risk while he avails himself of affordable fun with other women. Yalda feels an urge to go to the washroom.

Alone in the washroom, there is no need to worry about disguising the sound of her peeing. Although she's used to suppressing it for her own sake—either by targeting the side of the bowl instead of straight into the water or by flushing first—right now she tells herself that a tipsy woman doesn't deserve anything nice. She also tells herself that the sound can be the background music for the unwanted memory of her failed love affair, not only with Dan in Toronto, who talked about his wife as if she was a respected but not appealing female neighbour, but also with Marc in Springfield, who never talked about his wife, a stroke victim in a wheelchair.

To suppress her vertigo, Yalda pauses at the dim entrance of the bar. There is no quiet corner anymore. Without looking around, she staggers towards her table and picks up her scarf to leave. On her way to the cash, she bumps into the guy with the shaved head, who turns towards her. Her purse falls onto the floor and she loses her balance. The man, without leaving his stool, holds her with one hand and picks up the purse with the other. Before Yalda can utter a word, the man offers her the empty stool next to his.

9.

ONE LEG STRETCHED OUT, THE OTHER BENT. One arm folded under her breasts, the other half-looped around her head. Lying down on her stomach, she is mesmerized by an image: a swamp surrounded by an unknown forest. A frog rests on a lotus leaf. Out of the blue, a mild moonlit sprinkle turns to heavy, blinding rain. The dark curtain falls.

Yalda opens her eyes and jumps up. Allowing her eyes to get accustomed to the murky darkness, she looks around. She's on a burgundy sofa. Nearby, a window lets in feeble streetlight. She spots some white curtains, in various sizes, piled here and there in the cluttered space. On the opposite side of the room, there are some blurry posters and marionettes hanging on the wall. A shabby studio, she thinks. She shakes her head to ignite her memory. It must be his place, the man with the shaved head in the pub … the man who turned out to be a shadow player. *But where is he now?* She stands up to get a better view. In a murky corner of the room she sees the man lying in bed on his back. She holds her breath for a moment to hear better. His slow breathing tells her that he's in a deep, intoxicated sleep. She should leave before he wakes up. She sits on the edge of the bench. How did she end up here? She recalls that, when they arrived last night, she collapsed onto this bench seat, the first unoccupied space she had spotted.

At the pub, while raising his mug and making a toast, he'd introduced himself as a travelling shadow performer.

"A shadow man, eh?" she asked, not taking her eyes off her glass or expecting an answer.

"A puppeteer," the guy corrected her with his deep, but soft, voice.

It's my turn to correct you, she thought. But she decided not to. Let him judge her ability to comprehend English based on her accent. Nevertheless, her thoughts betrayed her, and slipped out of her mouth anyway. "The fact that you are not armed is enough for me right now," she said.

"Enough for what?" He sounded interested. He didn't turn to her, though.

She felt like having another drink to banish the disturbing thoughts from her head. "I don't know ... maybe enough to take revenge on him ... by sleeping with you," she replied sarcastically. Sitting side by side, they made no eye contact. Both of them fell silent, drowning in their own worlds. Heads bowed down, eyes fixed on their own drink. Wordless understanding.

"Hmm, sleep with me as revenge?"

"Nope," she muttered, not only to the shadow man, but also to the boy to whom she'd given birth—the boy to whom she had given all the love she had in the world.

"Lovers are betrayers," he added.

"Not my lover," she grumbled. "I'm talking about my son."

"Come on!" said the man after a long pause. He looked confused, shocked even.

"Shut up!" she replied, though not angrily. When she looked up and asked for another drink, the man inclined his head towards her.

"You've had enough," he warned in a decisive voice.

She opened her mouth to protest, but no words came out.

"Time to go home," said the man. "You'd better pay your bill and we'll go."

For a moment, that devastating cry filled her ears again. "I don't want to go home," she mumbled. "I don't want to get hurt."

"Does he beat you?"

"Of course not," she whispered. "But he ... he hid his life, his thoughts ... his plan to work as an armed guard—an armed guard for an armoured vehicle, like those that transport large quantities of money for banks—he hid that plan as if I were nobody. Oh, yeah. I'm nobody in his life." She let tears roll down her face.

Another pause stretched into a long silence. Once again, each of them retreated into themselves.

"Another glass, please!" she asked the waiter, trying to look convincingly sober. After the first gulp, she felt steady enough to prove that she was a woman in her right mind. "Let the world go to hell. But we should stay away from guns," she said, feeling her words disappear into a vacuum.

After a few moments of silence, the man responded, "You need to think differently, change your attitude about this, and maybe you will not feel so hurt."

Unable to recognize if he was being sarcastic or not, she turned to him. "Violence can not be erased with violence—I'm telling you."

"Go home and tell that to your son!"

Swallowing his bitter words, she replied, "I won't. Let me sleep over at your place—just tonight—and instead ... instead I'll tell you a tale that may work for you. I mean for your performance."

"Well, that's something," he said.

She took a last gulp of her drink, and continued. "Yes, I do have a tale for you, shadow man."

"Well, tell me," he said, heading towards the exit.

On the way, she called up all her mental energy and began. "Listen! Ever heard of *The Canticle of the Birds*? It's a tale told by a Sufi. And it goes like this: "A band of birds heads towards the Mountain Qaf. Why? Well, they're longing to find the mysterious bird, Simorgh. You know, Simorgh literally means thirty birds. What happens next? Oh! It's a long, long story. In the end, the thirty birds that were able to endure the hardship of the journey arrive at their destination and realize that they themselves are the Simorgh."

Yalda remembers telling him the story. As they walked, she stumbled several times, and each time he stopped so that she could regain her balance and keep going. He walked with slow, steady steps and avoided asking any questions. The cold evening wind made the few passersby bend their heads. She followed his bare, upright head. She could find no reason to question what she was doing.

10.

ODDLY ENOUGH, THE KEY, ALWAYS HARD to get into the keyhole and turn, doesn't give her any trouble tonight. A bonus for a drinking binge, she thinks. Her son's absence is another bonus. Lingering for a while in the hallway to remove her coat and scarf, she ruminates over the experience of opening the door and feeling relieved that he is not home. A wave of anger overrides the alcohol in her bloodstream. She throws her purse on the rocking chair and tramps toward the kitchen sink to drink a glass of water. When she feels she cannot drink any more, she splashes some water on her face. Before slogging to bed, she glances around. No sign of the jinn, which is good. She removes her clothes and collapses on her bed.

Yalda knows she should cover her eyes and summon flocks of sheep. She is hoping that the residue of alcohol will suppress nightmares. Before she pulls the blanket over her face, her eyes fall on the jasper green curtain, the partition between his room and her den. The curtain evokes a feeling of nostalgia for her childhood. She moves her eyes down and sees the jinn's shoes at the bottom edge of the curtain: black high heels, the tips of the toes, pointy and curled up. "Hey, you're here," Yalda snickers and closes her eyes.

I'm dreaming of something I experienced long ago. It's the first death, the first loss, the first bang *that goes straight through the heart of a young me, little Yalda. We're in Mati's room. I see the little girl's eyes, my eyes, wide open with horror, riveted by Mati's pale face. Mati is lying in bed, motionless and breathless, her head tilted toward her right shoulder, a lock of black hair stuck to her forehead, a single drop of blood oozing from the corner of her mouth. The aroma of eucalyptus leaves heating in a copper bowl of water mixes with the smell of Mati's medicine. All the sash windows of Mati's room are closed. The dark orange sunset turns the patterns of the lace curtains into bloody flowers. Little Yalda dashes to open the windows and screams as loud and long as she can. Nobody is home. Maman Ashi has gone to visit Sister Eti after her latest quarrel with our dad, Agha Jun, last week. Agha Jun never comes home after work when the lady of the house is absent. And Dadashi always goes out after he picks up little Yalda from school and takes her home. Weeping and wailing, this poor little me sits on the windowsill, her clenched fists knocking her head, her restless legs kicking the wall.*

The sun sinks behind the opposite roof; as it departs, the brick-paved inner yard, the symmetrical garden beds with their twin persimmon trees burdened with ripe fruit, and the rectangular blue-tiled pool, the howz, *are all drowned in darkness.*

"Mati, Mati, the day is done. Mati, Matiti, the day is done!"

Little Yalda laments. But Mati, the shining moon, Mati, her sweet elder stepsister, cannot be a refuge for her anymore. Her irrepressible sobbing reminds me of the jinn.

Yalda opens her wet eyes and removes the blanket from her face. She wipes away her tears with her pillowcase, and the water flowing down her nose with the edge of the bed sheet. Her short-term memory guides her to turn towards the jasper green curtain. No shoes, no hooves. An eerie moan from the opposite corner makes her turn around. The jinn, squatting, has covered her feet with her long black skirt. She has removed her high heels with their pointy, curled up toes.

Yalda wants to say, "*So you're going to stay here?*" Remembering her usual lack of tact, she resists saying anything unkind. The jinn has her hand over her mouth to suppress her blubbering. Yalda fails to find words of consolation.

BUT THIS IS A DREAM!

A very old dream. A dream that she experienced after the loss of Nader, her boyfriend, and Yunes, her brother. After Mati's death, Yalda often wished to see her in dreams. Sometimes, she could spot a phantom of Mati in some of the mishmash, those collages where you find the most irrelevant people in the most inappropriate settings. Never alone; never enough. Over the years, Mati has visited Yalda in her dreams twice, when she was mourning the loss of others, each time in one continuous dream that lasted for seven consecutive nights. The first time, Mati appeared to tame a Fury whose beloved man had been shot to death for nothing. The second time, though, Mati came to grieve with Yalda over their dear Dadashi, who had nothing in common with the murder victim in the morgue other than a name. After that, Mati disappeared, just like the jinn disappears—with no tinge, no trace, no smoke—as if Yalda had never had a half-sister who was as complete as a full moon. A wave of embarrassment runs under her skin.

"Mati, Matiti Juni, you're an unforgettable shining moon," she says out loud. She closes her eyes to let hot tears fall over her face, smiling for her missing moon.

As her hand reaches the edge of the sheet, she hears the jinn sniffling. She wipes her nose and gets up to remove the sheet. Avoiding eye contact with the jinn, Yalda gives her the crumpled sheet and drags her feet towards the washroom.

When she's back with a new sheet and an extra pillow, the jinn and Yalda catch each other's eyes. The jinn has now lifted her chin from her locked knees, clasping the crumpled sheet in her hands.

"It's not the right time for us to have Mati. Right?"

The jinn doesn't reply. Yalda ignores her *hamzad*'s icy stare and sloppily spreads the clean sheet on the mattress. Instead of lying on her abdomen, she sleeps on her side with knees curled towards her stomach, a pillow between them. She covers her body up to the neck with the blanket. Just like her son, she thinks, in a fetal position, covered up to the neck.

"I thought my jinn appeared because of my son, not because of my sister," she addresses the jinn.

The jinn jiggles her head and starts biting her nails.

"Mourning a lost sister is far better than cursing a degenerate son," Yalda taunts.

All at once, it occurs to Yalda that the jinn's reappearance might have to do with Mati after all. It makes the most sense. After all, it was Mati who'd made the jinn acceptable company for her. Although Yalda heard about the jinn from her mother, it was Mati who told Yalda that the jinn was not grotesque as Maman Ashi had described, with hooves, pointed ears, and a bald head. Instead, Mati told Yalda that the jinn was like an ordinary girl.

"So, the jinn is not a monster?"

"Not your jinn." Mati's smile was reassuring. "Yours is just like you. It's your *hamzad*. She was born when you were born, but in the jinn world. You don't believe what your wise half-sis says?"

"It's hard to believe, Mati."

But Yalda didn't doubt Mati for long. The moment Yalda saw Mati's sincere smile shining from her moon-shaped face, a shadow of a doubt fell on Maman Ashi's authority and credibility.

Maman Ashi had claimed that the jinn—a male creature with hooves, pointed ears, and a bald head—would penetrate into her youngest daughter's skin. Sick and tired of Yalda's whining, she used to say, "Aye! There is a jinn under Yalda's skin. That's what makes her mewl and yowl all the time." If anyone seemed doubtful, she would conclude that having such a difficult child was God's punishment for her bad marriage.

Later on, after Agha Jun's death, Yalda recalled that her mother's remarks about their marriage drove her dad crazy. Whenever Maman Ashi brought it up, Agha Jun would shake his ivory-handled cane in the air. The magic of his dancing cane was that it made Yalda stop crying in an instant. It also allowed Maman Ashi to breathe a sigh of relief that the jinn had disappeared. And it meant that Agha Jun was on his way out the door, which made everybody happy. Despite this, all three of them—Mati, Dadashi, and Yalda—felt guilty as soon as he had left the room, each for their own reasons.

With little sympathy for Agha Jun, Mati agreed with Dadashi that it was Maman Ashi who ignited the quarrel. Mati couldn't help being thankful to her generous stepfather who didn't complain about the over-the-top demands and expenses of his unhealthy stepdaughter. The bond between Dadash Yunes and Agha Jun was a different story. In his words, Agha Jun was a marshmallow trapped inside a walnut shell. While inside he was soft and sweet, on the outside he was severe and hard, like the tooth-breaking shell. But who put the sweet soft stuff into the tough shell? First, the bird-headed rural nanny who was hired by Agha Jun to take care of his two-year-old son after the death of his wife, and second Maman Ashi, the new wife of Agha Jun, who made him cautious about showing attention and affection to his only son.

When Yunes returned from the country house to his father's Tehran house to go to school, he had chronic hemorrhoids and some burn marks on his back. While he had been away, his father had remarried, so the motherless boy arrived in Tehran to find two new members of the household: a stepmother and a stepsister. From day one, there was a warm rapport between him and Mati, and a cold war between him and Maman Ashi. Agha Jun's new wife was a "high-born lady." Her full name, Ashrafolsaltaneh, was proof of her true or false affinity with the Qajars, the former royal family. All three children would hear, on and off, Maman Ashi complain about marrying an old man with no trace of nobility in his background and ever-shrinking wealth.

The jinn is shaking her compact body in a rhythm. She looks like an old woman in mourning. Yalda doesn't remember if Maman Ashi ever mentioned anything about jinns aging, but her *hamzad* is getting old.

Now that it's clear the jinn doesn't intend to bug her with a new mess, Yalda feels like talking with her.

"I'm telling you, tonight's dream was not the same as the one I already had," Yalda says. "I mean, this one was a bit different. This time you didn't show up—not you, and not anyone else."

In the old dream, the jinn had appeared to her from behind the curtain between Mati's room and Dadashi's, right at the moment she took her eyes from Mati's dead face. The jinn had loomed in front of her and disappeared in a second, as if she had no intention other than showing Yalda how to scream.

"There was another difference, though," Yalda continued.

As the little sister of Mati and Dadashi, and as a child with a limited attention span and zero restrictions from her parents, she knew many things partially or completely unknown to her peer group. No, death was by no means a mystery in her world. Confusing? Sickening? Maybe. Yet not secretive. Death was seen by Maman Ashi as an obnoxious angel with a special mission to make her a widow, by Agha Jun as God's executioner with no sense of punctuality, and by Dadashi as an eagle, always ready to swoop down on the newborn babies of his ignorant nanny, who never gave up the marathon of serial pregnancies. More than anyone else, however, it was Mati who had a connection with death—when she looked safe and sound; when she was in bed coughing and bleeding; when she was alive; when she was dead. She had talked about death as a part of life.

"Oh yeah, in the old dream I felt somebody come and sit

beside me while I was on the edge of the window frame. I'd seen Mati lying dead in her bed, but the arm circling around my shoulder could only be Mati's arm. I didn't turn my head at all. Instead, I closed my eyes, yielded myself to the soothing caress, and stopped weeping and wailing."

Yalda swallows the lump in her throat and grabs the hanky crumpled on the jinn's knees. She wipes her nose with it and leaves it on the floor beside the bed, in between her and her *hamzad*.

"Old or new, it's just a dream. Right?"

The jinn, still biting her nails, shakes her head a full one hundred and eighty degrees to indicate she doesn't know the answer.

"So, let's listen to Mati's story, okay? I know it by heart."

The jinn, twitching her head, reminds Yalda of a few rhymed words Dadashi and Yalda sang for Mati when they asked for her stories. "Mati, Mati, take off your veil! You're not a male! Tell us the tale!"

And then Mati would open her delicate mouth. When she was not in a storytelling mood, she would tease them. "I do have a tale, with a fly as a head, with a fly as a tail. Shall I tell it, or shall I not tell it?"

"Tell it! Tell it!" Dadashi and Yalda would entreat.

"I don't understand 'tell it, tell it.' I do have a tale, with a fly as a head, with a fly as a tail. Shall I tell it, or shall I not tell it?" Mati would continue.

"Not tell it! Not tell it!" Dadashi and Yalda would implore.

"I don't understand 'not tell it, not tell it.' I do have a tale, with a fly as a head, with a fly as a tail. Shall I tell it, or shall I not tell it?"

But if she was in a good mood, she would tell them her tale, always starting with the same opening.

"*Thus begins the tale of Mati, a baby girl born on a moonlit night. Her father named her Mah-e taban, which means the shining moon, since he saw the shining moon brightening her* face. Mati did not live under a lucky star, and she soon lost her father. Her mother, Maman Ashi, thinking herself a highborn woman, knew only one way to make a living: by having a man do it for her. For a woman who had been married twice and widowed twice, a third husband seemed out of reach. So Mati's mother moved in with her daughter and son-in-law. His house was like a stone castle for Mati. Such was the beginning of Mati's tough time living under Sister Eti, her elder stepsister. But the earth turns and change comes. Maman Ashi found a third husband and Mati found the second series of step-people: stepfather, stepbrother, stepsister. Poor Mati was surrounded by steps—some short, some tall, some big, some small. Well, what could she do? Nothing. After all, she, herself, was a step-someone, trapped in a step-world with no trace of anything proper, anything pleasing, anything palsy-walsy...."

Mati ended the story differently each time.

"So let me tell you one of the stories of one of the steps around us. For instance, you, our stepbrother. You, our Dadash Yunes. You, our Dadashi. Let me tell little Yalda how you welcomed me by throwing a wiggle-eyed frog into my chest. Or how you frightened little kids in the alley with your Dracula mask. Or how you tied a small purse of valerian to the tail of the neighbour's cat to make him dance around.

"And if you don't like that story, I can tell you one about another step, say, this little sis, this little Yalda, this little sweetie..."

"And if you don't like this story, my dear *hamzad,* I shall tell you the fucking story of a fucking woman with a fucking son and a fucking jinn under her skin...."

Yalda bursts into sobs, pulls the blanket over herself, and presses her face into the wet pillow.

11.

"SO, WHERE DO I GO FROM HERE?" she asks under her breath and hits the brake out of the blue. In the mirror, she can see the garage door closing behind her. As long as it doesn't move up for another car coming out, she can stop right here to figure out what she's going to do. She repeats the question, this time in her mind. She hears "dunno, dunno, dunno," inside her head—not her own voice, but a choked voice, possibly the voice of her jinn. She misses her. Too bad her *hamzad* can't bear the daylight. After everything, Yalda had a good feeling last night, having the jinn as company. It was a bizarre gathering of one who was dead, her *hamzad,* and a trapped animal that happened to be called Yalda.

Once, she had been Yalda Negunbakht (a surname that meant "bad luck"). So, she had changed her surname to Yeganeh (it meant "unique"), in the hope of avoiding any sinister omens. Thinking of this now makes her smile.

"Take me wherever you like, my silver horse!" Yalda murmurs, holding the middle part of the steering wheel.

She closes her eyes and imagines herself caressing the neck of a horse. She had never owned a horse, but had always longed for one. A tidal wave of longing for bygone days, when man could ride animals, rises up in her and forms a lump in her throat. She has hardly swallowed it when an image flickers through her mind: horseback riding on narrow paths that wind through a lush country garden. All three of them on a slim, trained horse—Dadash Yunes in the middle, Mati at the back, and Yalda in the front.

It was the last summer they had with Mati, a summer later named "Mati's summer." It was a time when all three of them were together, enjoying their vacation. There was no school during the day, and Agha Jun, who was in Tehran for business, was not there to torment them during the evenings. He had rented a garden house in Fasham for the entire summer, on the recommendation of Mati's doctor who'd prescribed mountain weather. She could have been sent to a special sanitarium for those afflicted with tuberculosis—it would have been less expensive—but Mati had not wanted to go, and asked instead to go to the garden house.

Yalda opens her damp eyes and changes gears. Around noon, when she got up, she felt an urge to go for a drive with no destination, to flee from the confines of the apartment. She needed a break from pretending there was no messy room, no messy son, no messy mind. Without a doubt, her silver horse does its job whenever she comes up against a blank wall. It is used to taking its helpless rider to random places, where she can kill time, though she must eventually admit that it is time that kills us.

Turning onto Post Road, she slows down out of habit. She wonders if she does this because of the speed bumps or because she wants to take a look at the grand mansions that line the road. They are in a variety of styles, from Greek to Gothic to Futuristic. She has to admit that she has never aspired to own or even design one of these mansions. Once she was a Frank Lloyd Wright aficionado and dreamed of designing a Usonian house.

Nader, her boyfriend, had called this aspiration, "An oblique dream of a perverse architect." When he made this remark, they had been celebrating their romantic reunion in a cozy restaurant in midtown Tehran. It was the fall of 1978. His seemingly sarcastic tone had annoyed her and she had stopped chatting and laughing. But her Nader, a political prisoner who had been recently freed from the Shah's prison, had an argument to make.

"Don't get me wrong, honey. After a year of dreaming about you, I like to see a big smile on your face. I'm not interested in a kiss that is not sincere."

Yalda tried not to laugh, knowing that his kiss would be a modest peck, but hoping he would continue.

"It's not that anything is wrong with your dream. But look around us and see what's happening," he clarified.

Yalda didn't pay much mind to politics, and at first she didn't get his point.

"Well, it looks like a revolution. I'm not a political person, though." She paused. "All I know is that thanks to this revolution, you don't have to spend years and years in jail for being an anti-Shah dissident."

Her Nader stretched his arms towards her hands, which were still moving in the air, and said, "Tell me Yalda, do you believe that?"

"I'd rather talk about my dreams tonight." She smiled, letting her hands be covered by his big ones, and kissed by his warm lips. "If you don't want a dream house, let's talk about another castle in the air."

"We're all wrong, our generation. It's not just the wrong time, it's also the wrong place, Yalda. If everything goes wrong.... I mean, what's coming is scary," her Nader said, ignoring the dirty look of a man at the next table who'd seen them kiss, and keeping her hands tightly in his.

"You don't sound like that sunny young man I used to know, my Nader!"

She clenches the steering wheel and shakes her head to send the memories of her Nader's back into the recesses of her mind. That all my darling dead ones are coming to me means that I'm indeed having another nasty problem, she thinks. To distract herself from disturbing thoughts, she has to replace her bag of dreams and nightmares with a bag of tricks. The most accessible trick is to immerse herself in the wonders of fall foliage on both sides of Leslie. The driver of a car behind her honks his horn. She is driving too slowly. She waves an apology while cursing him in her heart for interrupting her. She makes up her mind to go to Edwards Gardens for a stroll.

Despite the intermittent chilly breeze, she prefers to see the garden at this time of year, when it's quiet. When she had first come to Toronto, her host had suggested she visit this garden. It was the first time she had gone sightseeing in the city. She did it for her son, then a ten-year-old, still sort of on a leash. Unable to compete with his favourite parks, the garden didn't appeal to him. Soon afterwards, Nader discovered ravines and lost interest in the parks that he had once loved. She wonders if it was around that time that he lost interest in her as well.

After walking for an hour, she finds an empty bench with a view of the duck pond. As she is digging out her water bottle, she feels her cell phone vibrating in her coat pocket. "It's definitely not Nader," she says loudly, trying to quell her desire to hear his voice. She takes her phone out, turns it off, and sighs in frustration. On such a monstrous planet, she thinks, the only person who calls me is Jimmy, the ninny! She sometimes blames herself for expressing her anger by disgracing people with contemptuous titles. This time, though, she has no regrets. Once, in response to his insistence, she told him that men who undress all women in their minds cannot make women undress at all. Gazing at her in annoyance, he had grinned and said, "Who knows? You might change your mind."

The scenery in front of her eyes, unlike the scene in her mind, is comforting: a pale sky with strolling clouds. The weeping willows around the pond are drooping towards their shadows, and mallards are paddling around, indifferent to the passersby who linger to watch them. She spots a small child, with a parent on each side, trying to feed timid ducklings. From a distance, she cannot tell if the child, in blue pants and a yellow coat, is a boy or a girl. Boy or girl, the child's wavy hair reminds her of Nader's when he was the same age. She came to the garden to try to focus on the outside world, but everything reminds her of her son.

In Tehran, the well-manicured Niavaran Park would never be busy on an October weekday afternoon. Weekends were different, for the park had to embrace not only local visitors, but also those coming from the poor neighbourhoods in downtown Tehran to take advantage of the privileges granted to them by the revolution, including enjoying public spaces that had once been covertly exclusive. The park was situated at the foot of a royal palace, and it was now in the hands of those who had overthrown the monarchy. Niavaran Park was different from other parks. Even with the post-revolution inclusiveness, it had kept its pre-revolution name. No new name, no disguise, no false identity. Long ago, sitting on a bench with her back to the palace, Yalda had stared at the yellow fall foliage. She had wondered how the changed names of streets and parks had been destructive to her memory, her mind, her soul. That this park was still called Niavaran meant something. It was 1991. It was just a couple of days before Dadash Yunes was murdered, but she'd had no idea that was coming, and she was thinking about the good old days of meandering through that park with her Nader, her first love. That park had kept part of her past alive for her. It still evoked the melody of a Beatles song, "That Means a Lot," which then had been their favourite. It meant that after sixteen years, visiting the park with her son, a four-year-old Nader, she was able to recall how wonderful, how fresh, how young the newly built garden had been when she was fresh, when her Nader was young, and when their love was wonderful.

AND IT WAS NOT A DREAM.

Now, in 2008, although she is so far removed from the sixteen-year-old Yalda dating her first boyfriend and worrying about being caught by Dadash Yunes, she can still feel the Niavaran Park of 1975. But it's the Niavaran Park of 1991 that has become the setting of one of her recurring dreams.

In her dream, Yalda sits on a bench, but she doesn't look at either the monument or the water. She's there to watch her little boy walk and jump and run around, discovering the wonders of the park. Other than seasons that vary for no clear reason, another variable element in her dream is the presence or absence of Little Nader's father, Piruz, Yalda's ex-husband. When present, Piruz is busy chatting with a friend at the tea hut or following one of the paths. Just like his father, Little Nader goes any direction he likes and makes his mom breathless and tired running after him. She can never relax on a bench for very long. As soon as Yalda finds herself daydreaming, she notices that little Nader is missing. Running and sweating in a panic, she hears voices blaming her for not keeping her Little Bird safe. But Nader never gets lost; instead, Yalda is the one who loses her way.

She opens her eyes and sees a garden that is getting colder. The sun is lost in thick layers of gathering dark clouds.

12.

GOODNESS! WHAT AM I SUPPOSED TO DO? This thought, like a needle stuck in a groove, doesn't leave her alone. Over the last few days, she's thought about how to discuss the issue with Nader when he's back from camping, but she doesn't know how to approach it. The more she thinks about it, the less she has decided. The real issue is that it'll be hard, if not impossible, to have a discussion.

I know Nader will be deaf to all advice, Yalda thinks. Only an ineffectual mother would not be able to have a discussion with her son, she continues, berating herself.

While the first thought makes Yalda disappointed, the second one makes her angry. And this mix of disappointment and anger in her body causes a sudden rush of blood to her head and ears. To fight it, she decides to keep herself busy by doing a physical activity—not a pleasing one, a punishing one.

She zips by the closed door of the forbidden room and enters the bathroom to start her cleaning therapy with the toilet bowl. Her cleaning style requires a challenging posture: half-bent, one hand on her waist, the other holding the brush and moving at double speed to get the chore out of the way.

Today is different, though. She cannot follow her usual style. She pulls aside the shower curtain so that she can sit on the edge of the bathtub. She tries to focus on the task at hand, but the real mess is somewhere far away, completely out of her control. "God, what am I supposed to do with such a mess?" She holds her breath, hoping to hear a response from heaven.

Zilch!

Little wonder God doesn't bother himself answering; she only thinks of God when she is in a tight spot. In her right mind, Yalda is impartial enough to understand why God is always deaf to her words. If she is not mistaken, what urged her to seek help from God the first time was the chronic constipation of her little Nader.

For better or worse, the idea of God's help hadn't occurred to her when her Nader was in jail, either during the Shah's era or during that of the *mullahs*. Based on the simple logic of an atheist like Yalda, God should not be expected to help a communist like her Nader. The case of an innocent little baby suffering from a very trivial problem was different, though. A real God—not Allah or Yahweh or Ahura Mazda, but a no-name God—could not ignore the pleas of a young mother who had found all laxatives useless when it came to her baby.

"I may not know how to help Nader, but I know what to do with a toilet bowl," she mutters under her breath.

Having flushed the toilet to wet the sides of the bowl, Yalda applies a generous amount of powder to it. The cleaner's strong smell fills her nostrils, and she pinches her nose to block it out. She closes her eyes, reliving a memory.

"Time to go to the loo, Little Bird, before bed," Yalda said, wearing an encouraging smile.

Her sweet son didn't move. He just kept his nostrils pinched to convey a wordless message to his mom.

"There is no bad smell over there, honey."

No response.

"My Little Bird's pee and poo smell awesome." Her smile widened to make her words convincing.

Still, no signal.

"Come on, baby!" she said, her tone becoming strained.

There was no change in either his gesture or his stare.

She opened the bathroom door and turned on the light, trying to keep a trace of her fading smile. Her tough boy remained a stone statue. She asked her husband for help.

"Take it easy," Piruz responded, without taking his eyes off the evening news.

"Look, when this baby gets constipated..."

Piruz interrupted her. "Saddam is bombarding us..."

It was her turn to interrupt him. "Not us, not you. At least not yet. Now I'd rather think about my baby's urgent problem...." Her sentence trailed off, curtailed by Ahangaran's *noheh*, or elegy. Ironically, the mawkishness of the regime's singer reminded her of pre-revolution female cabaret singers. Not knowing where to direct her anger, Yalda tried to swallow it. Then, as a small revenge, she picked up Piruz's expensive *eau de cologne* from the cabinet and sprayed it in the air. Grinning again, she stretched her hand towards her dearest son. He let go of his nose and moved towards her inviting hand.

Yalda opens her eyes and takes her fingers from her nose. The powder still needs to sit for a while. She recalls that whenever she used *eau de cologne* to encourage her Little Bird to use the bathroom, she would miss Mati. That her little Nader couldn't stand the smell of his own poo reminded her of Mati, who had zero tolerance for any bad smell. The first time she noticed this resemblance, she got very excited about there being a trace of Mati in her son. Soon, her joy faded as the problems of parenting a toilet-resistant baby set in. Even so, she shared the story with Dadash Yunes in the course of their last conversation. It was an awkward conversation in Niavaran Park. When Yalda mentioned the *eau de cologne,* Dadash Yunes asked her what brand it was.

Hard to remember the brand after seventeen years, she thinks now.

It was the one Piruz wore before the revolution. Like all men of his class, he always used to dress up—unlike her Nader, who was always in jeans and casual clothes. After the revolution, Piruz stopped wearing suits and ties. There were no occasions for formal suits and ties anymore—no parties and no business meetings at a top-notch architecture firm.

Even so, he kept getting his favourite *eau de cologne*, either from the black market or from itinerant friends and relatives who were his supply line for goods from the Western world. While his rich collection of suits and ties—obsolete costumes of the Shah's era—was left abandoned in the closet, this *eau de cologne*, among a few other things, remained. It survived the *mullah*-imposed lifestyle, to the extent that he even wore it when he was in the seclusion of his seaside tangerine orchard.

Smelling the cleaner in the toilet bowl, she remembers the brand name: Aramis.

Its sweet scent never appealed to her. It was first imprinted on her memory as an artificial smell indicating the presence of a shallow, superficial man: Sister Eti's husband, a typical technocrat of the Shah's time with an insatiable thirst for promotion and Westernization.

When she met Piruz, who was her first boss at her first job, Aramis became a bit more appealing. After their marriage, it had a neutral appeal, as an indispensable manly item of the bathroom cabinet. It was only later on that it revealed its magical power of persuasion by encouraging her little Nader to go to the toilet.

But Aramis was not just a motivational tool for potty training. In fact, it became a tool of revenge on a husband who refused to take equal responsibility in parenting.

And it was not only about parenting.

"Not a caring parent, not a cooperative husband," she mumbles.

That Piruz's priority was always himself had never been a secret. To be honest, at first, it had seemed like an advantage, especially in comparison with her Nader's disposition. It was time, or marriage, or both that made this become a disadvantage, and it took her a very long time to recognize the metamorphosis.

The realization that she could not fight it was more disappointing. All of a sudden, Piruz gave up working as an architect, sold his share to his partner, purchased an orchard by the sea, and left her alone to manage the family budget.

Yalda recalls how his response to her protests varied from promising a future fortune from a prosperous tangerine orchard to complaining about how unbearable it was dealing with clients who he called post-revolution parvenus. He would preach about the importance of individuality and deny accusations of egomania or haughtiness, admitting only that he was a bit eccentric. Eventually, she had no choice but to give up her protests. She couldn't help it. As it happens, a weak position has always been her lot. Yalda admits that she's always found it more comfortable than a strong position. But she would rather lose the game outright than give up.

Focusing on cleaning, she scrubs the bowl forcefully. When it looks sparkling clean, she flushes the toilet to rinse the brush. After a deep breath, she wipes the sweat from her forehead with the back of her hand. Before putting the brush back in its place, she accidentally drops it. Bending down to retrieve it, she notices the yellowish ring right beneath the rim of the toilet.

"Holy shit! What am I…?" Her thought is interrupted by the click of a key turning in the lock. Listening to her heart beating like a hammer, Yalda thinks it will never slow down.

13.

SHE CANNOT STOP HER BODY SHAKING and her teeth chattering, reactions that have little to do with the weather. With her warm winter coat and a big wool scarf wrapped around her head, cold can hardly be accused of causing this weird shivering. Furthermore, it is a windless October night.

Nature morte. There is not even a slight breeze, a gentle breath of air, a soft murmur among the dark leaves. In the dead of night, she is a nothing but an infinitesimal dot, ignored not only by heaven and earth, but also by her only son.

Yet this tiny dot, she senses, is a developing seed of anger that will grow as big as the earth. It will overturn heaven. She wonders whether her shivering is signalling an explosion of furious anger or indicating a tremendous effort to suppress it. She knows that she cannot and should not keep the anger in her body. In fact, she started venting during her discussion with Nader. But it was aborted by his typhonic anger, which always compels her to beat a retreat. She was forced to push back her anger, to hide it for all the dragging minutes of the afternoon and evening, through the deadly silence that followed the bloody battle. Neither side had been victorious. Unable to fall asleep, she made up her mind to creep out of the apartment.

And now, on a bench in the parkette across from her place, Yalda feels helpless, not knowing how to get the imprisoned demon out of her body.

Bang! Bang! Bang!

Calling up all her energy to open her mouth, she spots the jinn squatting under a park light a few metres away from her. Her half-open lips let out a soft sigh. The jinn, resting her chin on her knees and fixing her eyes on Yalda, is tapping her mouth with one hand and hitting her head with the other. Briefly, Yalda considers taking her anger out on her jinn, but soon she understands what the jinn is trying to tell her.

"Hmm! You're telling me to keep my mouth shut?" she asks with a choking voice.

The jinn nods her head.

"And to beat myself? Right?"

The jinn keeps nodding and tapping and hitting.

"And you're the same jinn who used to go under my skin when I was a little kid?" she asks with a soft voice. "The one who taught me to scream and cry?"

The jinn widens her eyes, still nodding and tapping.

Yalda narrows her eyes. "I see. Because he is my son, I have to shut up and let him go to hell if he likes." She closes her eyes, covers her mouth with both hands, and bends forward to lean her forehead against her knees.

Once again, I am lost in a blame game that I meant to avoid, she thinks.

Recreating their encounter in her mind, she feels her face suddenly get warm. Her head is besieged by a flood of disturbing words and impressions.

She only meant to explain that a job as an armed guard was not just a job, but a lifestyle. She wanted to prove that it was not the right career choice for her son. She hadn't been able to articulate this properly, though. She'd hardly finished her question when Nader lost his temper and shouted at her.

"How dare you poke your nose into my stuff? Have you ever heard of privacy?"

Suddenly, she was on the defensive and Nader was in control of the argument.

"I was not disrespecting in your privacy...."

"Bullshit."

"Shut up, Nader!"

"You look in my room. You spy on me. When will you stop this fucking old-fashioned parenting?"

"I just went into your room to straighten up, to clean up your mess, to put things back in their place."

"How many times have I told you I want to keep my room messy? I don't give a damn that people want me to be organized."

"I'm not people. I'm your mom...."

Remembering, Yalda can't help letting out a moan. Sitting back straight, she notices that the jinn, with her chin still on her knees and her hands wrapped around her legs, is napping. Under the burden of self-pity, Yalda continues to groan.

"My dearest son cheated me. He turned it around on me. He thinks he is smart to do such a thing to his mom. This all started when he dropped out of university last year. Oh, Nader, didn't you tell me you just needed a break to find out what you really wanted? I was foolish. I trusted him and kept my patience for a whole year, letting him spend his days and nights on his laptop, letting him keep his plans secret. Idiot! Idiot! Idiot!"

Feeling a suffocating lump in her throat, Yalda falls silent. She finds it hard to swallow the lump down. With clenched fists, she beats her belly, cursing it for producing this damned son.

She presses her lips together to stop her teeth from chattering and leans her forehead against the chilly bench. To avoid hitting herself, she circles her arms around her head. She closes her eyes, hoping to detach from everything and everybody, including herself. If she were lucky enough to have a good fairy, instead of a nap-taking ineffectual jinn, she would ask her to wave a wand and turn her into stone.

I hate it! I hate you!

Words carved in stone, and hidden for years. Now a helpless— but not hopeless—mother has no way out, other than seeing these stony words, chewing on them, and swallowing them.

Yalda suddenly remembers the summer of 1998, in Saint-Étienne. Nader was yelling, full of anger and hatred, "I hate it! I hate you!"

Nader was eleven years old. He had locked himself in their apartment, and he was shouting and kicking the door nonstop. Yalda was leaning her shaking body against the entrance of their small studio. It had become a barrier, a boundary, a border. It was a barricade made by Nader to proclaim that he was not his mom's Little Bird anymore. Since she'd announced that they were going to cross a border again, he had started to express his disagreement in different ways. Praying no one, particularly the landlord, would pass by in the hallway, Yalda had wiped her tears with a crumpled tissue. Nader could not damage the strong wood of the door in this old building, but despite its worn-out look, the building brought in big money for its owner and any mark could cause the greedy landlord to withhold their security deposit. Yalda knew she couldn't open the door by force and punish him. No punishment, even TV deprivation, worked with her stubborn kid. Yalda had no choice but to hope that he would stop his crazy behaviour soon.

A few days before, Yalda had been washing dishes as part of her job at a restaurant. She was trying to find the best opening for a tough discussion. She wiped her sweaty forehead with her sleeve and cast a quick look at the clock to make sure she would finish before Nader came back from school. Yalda didn't like her son seeing her wash the customers' dishes. When she'd said she was going to work part-time at a restaurant, Nader hadn't shown much interest, so she had avoided getting into the details. When she'd told him that her boss was their family friend, Uncle Ali, Nader had wrinkled his nose. At the time, Yalda had interpreted his reaction as an indication that he disliked the smell of *chelow kabab*, rather than Uncle Ali. Later, he'd refused to go to the restaurant after school, and insisted on going home alone, reluctantly promising not to watch TV in the afternoons. That morning, though, she'd promised to take him to a movie theatre after work. Her plan was to tell him about her recent decision and smooth things over with a pleasant outing. She'd anticipated a mild outburst, but she'd been confident that she could calm him down by explaining and making promises about a better future. Now that the time was approaching, she was feeling more anxious about the possibility of a major storm.

In the storage room, she had tried to make herself look and feel like a decent mother, changing her sweaty T-shirt and putting on a perfume sample. But she sensed an impending hurricane. For a second, she considered all her other attempts to provide Nader with a better life:

1992: leaving Tehran forever and living in Essen for a year – Nader is five.
1993: leaving Essen and living in The Hague for half a year – Nader is six.
1994: leaving The Hague and landing in Saint-Étienne – Nader is seven.
1997: planning to leave Saint-Étienne and move to Canada – Nader is ten.

Yalda shook her head, trying to put their history out of her mind. When you make the earth beneath his feet quake, she thought, you deserve a hurricane. This thought didn't last long, though. It was replaced by an old image of her childhood, one that had recurred to her from time to time since she began wandering the earth with her Birdie: a stray cat moving her kitten from place to place, changing locations in search of safety.

She put a bowl of salad, a plate of saffron rice with crunchy rice crust, and a can of Coke on the table, "Are you sure you don't want kabab, *mon chéri?*" she asked her son.

As he was wrinkling his nose, she sat down. She could have taken him to a restaurant, she thought, if she'd been sure how he would react.

"I know you don't like to eat here, *mon petit oiseau*"—she chose words carefully—"but we have to rush a bit to arrive at the theatre on time."

He didn't seem to have much of an appetite, and Yalda could tell that he had probably already had something. Yet it was not the right time to preach about the disadvantages of eating snacks. "Natalie is coming back soon," she said.

"Who's Natalie?" Nader asked with little interest, not taking his eyes off his plate.

"I'm talking about Uncle Ali's wife, *chéri*," Yalda responded. "You've already met her. Don't you remember?"

Nader shrugged his shoulders, so she clarified: "When Uncle Ali is out of town, she's my boss. I've taken the rest of day off, but we have to wait for her to come back from shopping."

When Nader opened the Coke and a trace of joy flickered across his face, Yalda thought it was the right time to get to the point.

"I have some news for you, Nader!" She swallowed her saliva. "Good news, I guess."

For the first time, Nader turned his eyes towards her and gazed at her in silence.

"I cannot find a job as an architect here, and I don't want to keep taking this or that *petit* job forever. My application for permanent residence in Canada has been approved ... so, we'll be leaving Saint-Étienne soon."

Nader interrupted her by closing his fists and beating them on the table. The can tipped over and the brown, bubbly drink overflowed. Yalda put her hand out and grabbed it, but the Coke spilled all over the table and splashed over her lemon-yellow dress—her only party dress. She couldn't help shouting and cursing. "*Putain! Toi t'es vraiment un garçon idiot!*"

Anxious to clean up before Natalie came back, she ran towards the kitchen to fetch a cloth. Coming back to the table, she noticed his cold, indifferent eyes. She wanted to make up with him, but he didn't give her a chance.

"I'm not coming. I don't want to move again." He forced words out of his cracked lips with clear antipathy.

"We have to," she muttered under her breath.

I hate it! I hate you!

Carved in stone. But covered with the dust of disregard.

Yalda feels an abrupt surge of compassion for her Little Bird in her heart. Her inner shaking has vanished, so she gets up to go back home.

14.

TEARS CASCADE DOWN HER WIND-BURNED CHEEKS, the product of two months' worth of frustration. Yalda can taste their saltiness on her cold lips. If not tears of joy, they are at least soothing.

"Goodness, I finally spoke out!" she says aloud.

A senior couple passes by and pauses. She presses her lips together to pretend she was not the source of sound. Attempting to keep the snot from running down her upper lip, she digs into her coat pocket for a used tissue. The couple, both shrunken, resume their slow walking. Yalda gives up on finding the tissue and wishes she had a lucky star—she's never had a man around to hand her a sparkling white handkerchief. As she watches the couple, she wonders if the elderly man has kept the manners of an old-fashioned gentleman, or if it is the poor old woman who is in charge of keeping her man tidy and clean in private and public. She brushes her tears away with the back of her hand, but she's reluctant to wipe her nose and make her hand dirty.

Too bad that the gust of wind is not cold enough to turn it into an icicle, she thinks.

It seems she has no choice but to use her scarf. She's a sort of casual clean freak, though, so after cleaning her nose and face and before stuffing the scarf into her huge purse, she rolls it up tightly so that the wet part cannot contaminate anything inside the bag.

As she heads towards the mall entrance, she remembers she didn't give Nader any advice about driving safely. Not that he would take it. Knowing well that mom's advice is neither heard nor welcome, Yalda is reluctant to advise him. Yet the advice about safe driving is an exception; she can't help giving it. She knows, though, that no matter what she means by it, he interprets it as a warning about misusing her car or incurring extra costs.

He doesn't give a damn about my obsessive parental worries, she thinks.

Nonetheless, some financial worries, like an insurance rate increase or expenses due to bad driving, somehow make sense to him; he doesn't make any disapproving gestures when she gives her recurring report about the tight family budget. When Nader was in school, she used to blame herself, overtly and covertly, for her inability to provide her only son with a comfortable life. Since he dropped out of university, though, Yalda took the blame off her back and put it on his. And now? Well, now the blame is being passed between a naïve mother and an ignorant son, each unable to understand the other.

"But I spoke out!" she says again, pushing the revolving door of the mall forward. Somebody behind her makes an abrupt lunge, and she hits her forehead against the door frame. She winces a bit and takes it as a sign that there is no reason to be happy. But as she begins to warm up, she feels more optimistic.

The mall, often quiet as a result of its low-traffic location, is now busy with Christmas shoppers. Its usual dull look has been spruced up with flashy Christmas decorations. She has no plans to shop, but she would like to hang around in a warm and safe place, contemplating her dilemma. Nader adamantly refuses to discuss his shocking decision to become an armed guard. If Yalda attempts to broach the subject, he insists on shutting the conversation down with a few words:

"Not your choice to make!"

Then, every time, he rushes to his room and slams the door behind him.

Today, though, Nader's tactic didn't work. Last night, when he asked about using the car to go to an interview, she took advantage of the opportunity. "I've been asking to discuss something with you for a long time...."

Oddly, she succeeded in keeping her voice soft and smooth.

"There's no point in discussing it. I've already told you what you should know," Nader said, trying to be as tolerant as he could.

"Yes, you have. But you haven't given me a chance to explain why I am against it," she said, surprised by her adequate word choice, something she was rarely able to do.

"Mom, I'm exhausted right now, and tomorrow I have the interview."

"I have my AutoCAD class tomorrow afternoon ... but you could drop me off at the mall nearby and pick me up at five."

"I spoke out," she says again, her eyes fixed on the fibreglass lips of a mannequin in a store window. But she acknowledges that it didn't help.

She didn't get any sleep the previous night, not because of the plan to express her thoughts to him, but because the words she would need to use, the appropriate words, for the moment eluded her.

To pass some time before her class starts, she heads to a coffee shop. She has so much on her mind that she's grateful she doesn't have to prepare for her class. Because her job is relatively undemanding, she is able to sip a coffee, nibble on a cinnamon cookie, and watch people engaging in their capitalistic Christmas rituals.

She chooses a spot far away from the occupied tables. With a slight twist of her head, she can keep herself occupied by watching the constant flow of people coming into the mall and passing her. Among the crowd she spots a young, very pregnant woman looking around blankly. Yalda savours her coffee and closes her eyes for a second, trying to picture herself when she was pregnant for the first and last time in her life. She can't seem to form an image of herself. Instead, she recalls how earnestly she tried to guess what her baby would look like; she would look at everyone she passed on the street, wondering if her baby might resemble them. For some reason, she had no interest in thinking about what her baby would look like when he was born. All she thought about was what he would look like when he was an adult. Would he be as thin and tall as the young man who had just passed her? Or as short and stout as the one coming towards her? Would he be handsome? Or slovenly, like most young men of the post-revolutionary era? Would he...? Suddenly she sees an image of Nader in a uniform, equipped with a gun. *Ça suffit!* She opens her eyes.

Yalda turns her head and notices a boy sitting on a bench with a big box next to him. According to the picture on the side of the box, it contains a war toy, yes, a plastic machine gun. His shoulders are tense, and his palms press against the bench on both sides of his thighs, and he is shaking his legs nervously. His colourless lips are parted, revealing a missing tooth. His blue eyes, staring at her, look like a fish's eyes—very cold and very blank. What is bothering him? she wonders.

A sense of awkward familiarity hits her, and a sudden shiver runs down her spine. Yalda takes her eyes off him and grabs a pen and paper from her bag to keep her hand and mind busy with doodling. As her hand glides over the blank sheet, her mind flies far away to the police headquarters in downtown Tehran.

Piruz drove all the way there, from the north of the city to downtown, and she'd been like a zombie the whole time. Not a word, or moan, or even a sigh had been released from her closed lips since Piruz had hung up the phone and asked her to follow him. The more he'd tried to be sympathetic, the less she was able to react to what had happened. While Piruz was on the phone, trying to fill in the blanks, Yalda found herself unable to conceive of two words together: Yunes and murder. Hearing them in the same sentence, her brain suddenly shut down.

Bang! Bang! Bang!

The words coming out of the homicide detective's thick lips were garbled and indistinct—the loud *bangs* reverberating in her head. Yalda wondered if she was paralyzed by the detective's unexpected words, or out of the fear that her head might explode.

"I asked you, Madame, would you like to take custody of the victim's children?" the officer said.

"Does she have a choice?" asked Piruz.

"Well, if your wife doesn't want to," the man turned his eyes to Yalda, "the children's maternal grandfather will have custodial rights."

"That obnoxious old man! It's not enough that he raised a murderer!" Piruz's words were sarcastic rather than angry.

So, Yunes was, in fact, murdered by his wife!

"The case is under investigation, sir."

"A man has been murdered." Piruz sounded calm and rational.

"True. The whole family had been detained," the cop said. "Other than the little girl, I mean."

Feeling the cop's curious stare, Yalda summoned all her energy to say something, but Piruz spoke instead. "Did she witness the murder?"

"They locked her in the bathroom so that she couldn't see or interrupt," the cop continued. "That's what they said. The boy hasn't opened his mouth yet. When the cops arrived after the woman's call, they found the little girl in the toilet—not the one in the building, but the one at the far end of the yard, close to the front door."

"Where is Iran now?" Yalda heard her voice as though it were coming from the bottom of a well.

"In the next room," the officer turned his head toward a closed door.

When Piruz opened the door for her, she leaned against the doorframe. Right across from her, Iran, sitting on a bench, her legs shaking nervously, had her shoulders forward and her palms pressed against the bench on both sides. Her missing tooth, revealed through parted lips, touched Yalda's heart. She wanted to step forward but she couldn't. The girl's blue eyes, fixed on her, had looked icy, and empty. On impulse, she turned to the high-ranking officer. "I want to see my brother, officer, wherever he is."

Her words, although surprising to her own ears, were articulate enough to get a nod from the man. She felt she had enough energy and love for the youngest survivor of her poor Dadashi, but when she was back in the officer's room, her sudden energy vanished. The cop began to speak, and she felt his words crashing over her.

"You can take the little girl out of here right now, but the boy should stay in detention. We suspect he was involved. His mother and twin sister denied his involvement. According to Sharia, his twin sister is considered an adult, and has been since she turned nine, but he is not considered an adult yet. As a male, he is not an adult until he turns fifteen, and that won't be for a couple of months yet. Hopefully he'll be let out, rather than sent to jail. If he denies his involvement or keeps his mouth shut, you can get custody of him."

Yalda notices the tip of her drawing pen has pierced the paper wherever she meant to mark a knot in her tangled lines. Without taking her eyes off of it, she repeatedly presses the pen into the page of her notebook, recalling the day the twins were born.

"Hurry up, Sis. We're going to be late. Queen Ensi and her newborn twins, Princess Turan and Prince Turaj, should be discharged from the hospital soon."

"Don't make me nervous, Dadash Yunes. Let me double-check my bag to see if I have everything."

"Don't be fussy, Sis!"

"You don't want your newborn twins to catch a cold, do you? And here are their blankets: the pink for my niece, and the blue for my nephew. So cute! Okay, I'm ready. Now we can hit the road in your new antique car."

"Cross your fingers and hope my Chitty Chitty Bang Bang doesn't get stuck along the way. I haven't had time to fix it since I picked it up at the used military car sale."

"Too bad! I was hoping to get few driving lessons now that you're in Tehran to make up for the last time you taught me. Ah! What a goof! I still feel embarrassed when I remember how I let the car get stuck in a ditch. You lost your confidence in my driving abilities, didn't you?"

"You just wanted to prove that your big brother is like Hercules. Don't worry about it. You have one more year to get your driver's license, right, Sis? You have to turn eighteen first. This coming Nowruz, you can come to our one-horse town to get stress-free driving lessons and babysit the twins."

"Won't you have visitors from Ensi's family over the holidays?"

"Oh, yeah, I will. On holidays, we always have a platoon of Ensi's siblings taking refuge in our house. They escape from the garrison Haji has made for his tribe. They have open mouths, not helping hands."

"But couldn't Haji's wife be of some help to her daughter? She's a first-time mom with twins, after all."

"Are you kidding? Thanks to Haji's generosity, my mother-in-law feels like an undernourished baby factory who needs a full-time caregiver. Her husband is stingy with his money, and doesn't provide her with enough food or help in the house."

"Okay. When your mother-in-law is not able to help, you can leave Ensi and her babies here with me. Now that Maman Ashi is gone, they can stay with me in the apartment. You pay the rent, after all; it's yours."

"Not a good idea, Sis. It doubles my expenses."

"I feel guilty, Dadash Yunes. I will leave school to get a job...."

"No, you won't. I don't want you to do what I did. I left school and now instead of operating planes, I repair them. If Mati were alive.... Anyway, I'm alive...."

"I don't want to be a burden for you, Dadash Yunes. I have just one more year until I get my diploma. I can go back to Sister Eti's."

"No way. I sacrificed my future so that you.... Anyway, you won't go back to that house. Don't forget Sister Eti's husband who claims he lost our father's fortune through bad investments."

"It was Maman Ashi who first screwed up your life. I know it, Dadash Yunes. You lost not only the inheritance, but also the chance to marry Turan, the girl you loved. Yet all these years you paid the rent for Maman Ashi and me so that I could live an independent life. Now it's time for you to take care of your family."

"Don't be silly, Sis. You are my family. I vowed to take care of you till you finish university. Then you can become a rich architect and build a mansion for your humble brother."

"But now you have a big family of your own!"

"Oh yeah! With this sudden double burden, I mean blessing, I'm up to my neck in debt. But that's not your problem. All you have to do is smile and be a nice auntie."

"And what about the first-time dad?"

"He can't help but frown over his miscalculations."

"What miscalculations, Dadash Yunes?"

"Sis, I wanted Ensi to deliver the babies in Tehran at a reliable hospital. I didn't count on any help from my father-in-law, Haji. I knew how stingy this obnoxious old man could be. Otherwise, how else could a doorman become a rich property owner who does nothing but collect rent and prayer beads? But I thought that maybe this time it would be different—different because it concerned the welfare of his daughter and grandchildren."

"You asked for money?"

"I asked for a loan."

"And?"

"He said if I'd been a wise man I would have planned a home birth with a local midwife and minimal expenses."

15.

NOT AWAKE, NOT ASLEEP. IN A TRANCE. *I feel as though I can transcend my physical body, but, at the same time, I am still myself, grounded and ordinary. The first standpoint gives me the hallowed authority of an invisible observer, sort of an ineffectual or indifferent God, who watches from his heavenly throne as a scene unfolds far below. The second is a replica of me, not a* hamzad *like the jinn, just a modest copy of Yalda in an obsolete frame.*

BUT THIS IS A DREAM.

The dining room, with its antique furniture, is spacious and luminous, crowded and smoky. Noise and smoke coming from the dining and poker tables pollute the air. Yalda is sitting on a corner sofa, far enough from these two hubs and close to a half-open window behind a lace curtain. Staring at her full plate, she puts it on a small mahogany table.
 It is Rasht, March '88. A wealthy client is hosting a bunch of frightened families who have fled the bombardment of Tehran.
 Yalda looks preoccupied, or disinterested in the conversation between Piruz, on her left, and Lady Liaison, on her right. Her Little Bird, who has just recovered from an allergy attack, is sleeping upstairs. Yalda would prefer to be with him, but before she can leave the gathering, she has an announcement to make.

"I will be going back to Tehran," Yalda says, filling a pause in the conversation between Piruz and Lady Liaison. "I'd rather die at home than stay here and kill time with a bunch of horror-stricken war refugees."

"That makes no sense to me," Lady Liaison declares. "But you have the right to be a war martyr, honey."

"Yalda and I have discussed the issue enough," Piruz says, exchanging a glance with Lady Liaison. "I'm just concerned about the baby."

"I can take care of my son," Yalda replies, taking a deep breath. "I suppose."

"Really?" Piruz snickers. "And where did you get your son from?"

"Piruz is right, honey," Lady Liaison pronounces. "Nobody in their right mind would believe that a baby, bastard or not, wants to be the victim of a war between devils."

Yalda steadies herself, determined not to lose her temper and fall into their trap. "This damn humid weather is not good for a baby with an allergy problem." She turns her face to Piruz. "He needs special care, and you're definitely not an attentive enough father to give it to him."

"Don't worry, honey. I'll take care of little Nader," Lady Liaison mediates. Then she raises her voice towards the poker table to address her husband sitting there. "You'll lend me a hand, darling, in taking care of our friends' baby, won't you?"

Piruz's business partner nods in reply. Everybody knows what this means: he recognized his wife's voice, but didn't pay attention to her words.

"Not father material at all," Piruz says coldly. Whenever he speaks this way, it always disarms his listener. "But I am a father who happens to live under the gracious auspices of Islamic fundamentalists. I am therefore entitled to disallow custody of my son to his foolishly adventurous mother..."

"Their benevolence reaches out to all types of mothers, dear Piruz," Lady Liaison interrupts him.

Piruz raises his hand in the air to signal the end of the discussion. As he stands up to head to the poker table, Yalda turns towards the window to avoid eye contact with anybody. The window has been opened by a damp wind. Yalda takes a breath of the fragrant Caspian night air to clear her throat before running upstairs.

But she does not reach the quiet, lamp-lit room where her Little Bird is sleeping.

Instead, she finds herself in a vast forest clearing under a grey midday sky. Piruz's business partner is walking alone. A few metres behind him, his wife and Piruz are discussing the war. As always, Lady Liaison's part in the conversation is dominant and decisive. And as always, Piruz handles the discussion in his own way—without many words, or much passion, but with unyielding stubbornness. It is the first day of their flight from bomb-stricken Tehran. The previous afternoon, Yalda was shocked not only by bombs falling over the city, but also by all the people—those who could afford to anyway—suddenly running away. They were leaving the capital to seek shelter in any town outside of the target area of Iraqi warplanes. Now Yalda wants to take part in the conversation about their forced evacuation, being careful not to look too disapproving, lest it be attributed to her reluctance to leave her home and her town. Yet her Little Bird, toddling around, doesn't let her adjust her walking pace to anybody's but his.

Little Nader is exploring his strange surroundings with a fresh sense of wonder. Walking and running in different directions, he pauses to watch and touch worms and insects. As an overly worried first-time mother, Yalda suspects that the wilderness is the perfect place for her fragile baby. She admits, though, that Lady Liaison was right when she said, "You cannot raise your child in a vacuum." Yalda wonders if their host's villa could be considered a vacuum from Lady Liaison's point of view. Suddenly she hears an odd sound from little Nader and finds him collapsed on the ground near a lush fern. Frightened, she *notices that his face is swollen and blue. Unable to cry, he is just making choking sounds.* Yalda opens her mouth to call Piruz, but rolls of fog slide into her mouth, becoming dense enough to clog her throat.

Then the scene changes: the forest clearing is replaced by a railroad. It looks like Essen railway station, but can't be anywhere other than the Rasht train station.

Sitting upright on the edge of a bench, Yalda recalls how she felt dense fog roll into her throat on the first day of their flight, at the first appearance of little Nader's allergies. Over the two weeks that followed, in the draining hours of caring for her sick baby and the irksome minutes of living life in a herd, she's decided to go back home with her son. Yet now, at the moment of departure, she is by herself, leaving her Little Bird in that villa with a self-absorbed father and a bizarre bunch of intellectual elites.

She can't help picturing the blue and swollen face of her helpless baby, the stamp of the previous night's nightmare. Shame, as thick as a layer of mud, covers and hardens the foggy stuff in her throat.

I'm nothing but a fucking coward, Yalda thinks.

Last night, after the awkward conversation about her decision, Yalda could have discussed the issue with Piruz when he came into their room to sleep, but she decided not to bring it up.

It wouldn't have worked; she is positive.

She could have swallowed her pride and begged him, or she could have played the role of Delilah to get permission to take her son back home.

But it wouldn't have done any good.

She had been browbeaten, and she trusted she would lose the battle as soon as Piruz asserted his legal child custody rights. Piruz had a strong claim: he didn't want to put his son's life at risk. He also had advantages: a proud, feminist, female accomplice who would offer to help with babysitting, and that macho Sharia law that protected vulnerable children from "unwise and immature" mothers.

That she didn't consider abducting her own baby was not because of the threat of Sharia. The Islamic law could only loom ghostlike over Yalda in a divorce court in Tehran, and it was not likely that Piruz would refer to a provincial court or the police. Instead, Yalda is worried about what she considers to be the most likely scenario: a couple fighting, a scandalous fuss in front of a group of nosy people looking for fun, an informal trial with Lady Liaison as the judge, and a verdict against her. I'd rather lose the battle than lose face, Yalda thinks.

To lose face would make Yalda extra guilty in the eyes of a judge like Lady Liaison, a powerful and confident woman who would no doubt feel contempt for anyone weak enough to be embarrassed publicly. In contrast, Yalda finds fault with Lady Liaison's emphasis on self-criticism. It reminds her of the radical anti-Shah opposition and its so-called ego-stripping sessions where self-criticism is overvalued.

The blame game doesn't fix the problem, though. She is ashamed of her own fear of losing face, which is rooted in a rigid traditional culture. It impedes her rights, and keeps her from blaming Piruz for taking advantage of what he likes to call "the stinky holes" of an Islamic regime. Though Piruz, in this way, expresses his contempt for the Islamic regime and Sharia law, he does not hesitate to use that same law to assert his rights, as Nader's father, to make final and binding decisions about their son.

A train whistle, loud and insistent, interrupts Yalda's thoughts and makes her appallingly aware that she is about to leave her baby behind. Trying to ignore the heavy feeling in her throat, she spots Lady Liaison coming towards her with her usual confident walk. A sudden beam of hope appears.

"So, you've made up your mind to try your luck at being an unwanted martyr," says Lady Liaison. Although her tone is not sarcastic at all, the beam of hope starts flickering. Praying not to burst into tears, Yalda remains silent.

"The host and I are going to town to go shopping for the war-phobic garrison that is our home. I asked him to stop by for a few minutes to see you," Lady Liaison continues with her air of pompous self-confidence.

The flickering beam brightens, and Yalda's face glows for a moment.

"At the breakfast table, Piruz said he couldn't find his car keys. Do you happen to have them with you?"

These unexpected words devour the beam. Yalda stretches her hand toward her throat after shaking her head no. Her hopes have been dashed. Lady Liaison has not come to tell her that Piruz has agreed to let her have her son.

"Okay. I have to go." Lady Liaison pulls her silk scarf over her jet-black bangs. "Enjoy your trip and don't worry about your baby. He'll be safe and sound here, far away from the madding crowd." As she disappears into the crowd, Yalda feels the lump in her throat dissolve into warm tears.

In the following scene, I, the God-like observer, don't see even a single teardrop rolling down Yalda's cheeks. Her eyes look solid and dry as two bony marbles; her face, though, is constantly changing.

A zombie at home; a ghost in a haunted Tehran. With no tears in her eyes and no voice in her throat, Yalda is looking for traces of a life that would have been lived, of time that could have been the past, but not the present, in a place that should have been home.

Instead, home smells like horror.

Yalda doesn't find her Little Bird in his bed, in the living room, in the kitchen, in the washroom, on the veranda, in the yard. She turns on all the lights, opens all the doors and windows, plays music from all their cassette tapes.

Horror has a hollow face.

Yalda doesn't find her neighbours, her friends, her relatives; they were all wealthy and wise enough to vacate a city that is losing residents and gaining rumours.

Rumours are sticky.

News of Saddam's gas attack on Halabja fills the citizens of Tehran with fear. The tragedy that they have already been through, the bombardment of the city, looks rather insignificant compared to what is yet to come: horrifying chemical weapons. Yalda wanders around the city with clenched fists hidden in the big pockets of her Islamic manteau. She stops at newspaper stands. The number of bombs is bold in the headlines; the number of casualties is lost between tiny, trivial words.

The streets are free of traffic, the sidewalks have no jampacked crowds, the sky bares its bright blue chest, and there is a fragrant breeze, but all of this is unable to bestow on Tehran the lovely face it used to have during the long Nowruz holidays.

Yalda rambles through the alleys and avenues, looking for the footprints of evil. There are no piles of corpses, no signs of any injured people, not even a war or ambulance siren.

Yet evil leaves traces.

She finds these traces where there is nothing, where the missiles destroyed a building and left it a vacant lot. She ends up in the nearest vacant lot to her home, the one attached to the bakery where Yalda often gets her bread. Without the building, the alley looks like a comb with a missing tooth.

That the bakery is closed with a huge metal lock on its door doesn't make sense. That only stray dogs and cats are around also doesn't prove anything. Furthermore, Yalda knows the newly constructed building well, not just because of its awful architectural style, but because of the corner balcony on the second floor.

The bakery offered the best *taftoon in the neighbourhood.* Often, Yalda could not help but put a chunk of bread in her mouth after waiting in the bakery's long line. As she munched on the fresh crispy bread, she would hear a sweet sound coming from the balcony.

"Ma, ma, ma, ma." A baby, with smiling brown eyes and wavy dark blond hair, babbling.

Well-dressed and safe in his buggy, he would move around the small space in between the wrought iron railing and the half-open door, which his mom peeped her head through every once in a while.

It was said that the building, a doll house in the dark, collapsed in a minute when the first missile struck. None of its dolls survived.

Nonsense.

Yalda can still see the baby. As he starts babbling and stretching his hands through the railing, she recognizes her own Little Bird.

It's a perfect balcony with a wrought iron railing, detached from the ground and sky, right up in the air, under the smelly, sticky rain of bombs and missiles. With her eyes fixed on a phantom looming in the distance, she identifies a troop of men, all in uniform, all headless.

Yalda opens her mouth to scream. Nothing but choking moans come out of her throat. Her hands, stretching towards the baby on the balcony, quiver. Sticky sweat covers her pulsating temples.

Wake up! You're dreaming. Wake up! Nader holds a glass of water to her lips and murmurs, "Relax, Yalda!"

Blinking her eyes in an effort to wake up, Yalda wets her dry lips. It occurs to her that her son has not called her "Mom" in a long time. As soon as her eyes meet his, she bursts into tears and starts hitting him with her closed fists.

"I can't stand the idea of seeing you armed with a gun," she whimpers.

Nader slams the glass on the bedside table. "You're crazy," he says with increasing volume. "Your ideas are coming from your lousy past, from your voodoo homeland, from your naïve mentality."

"Shut up! Shut up! Shut up!" Yalda hits her head and face hysterically.

"If I shut up," Nader sneers, "you'll keep acting like an uneducated and uncouth person, who doesn't understand law and order."

"Law and order! Is that what you're fed by the highly sophisticated American TV?" Yalda says, shaking her head and hitting it against the wall.

"I don't give a damn that your inner snob rejects the idea of me in a uniform," Nader says coldly and stomps off through the door.

"It's not about the uniform, Nader," Yalda moans. "It's about the gun that goes with it. It's about accepting violence as part of your daily life. It means you're ready to kill or be killed at any moment."

"That's just stupid and, anyway, I don't care what you think," Nader utters finally and slams the door.

Jumping out of bed, Yalda runs to the balcony hoping to douse her fiery anger in the cold of the February night.

16.

THE SCENERY BEFORE HER, the northwest corner of Yonge and College, offers a very common urban collage. Yalda, with her flair for erasing undesired dots and lines, empties it of people, signs, words—unwanted forms and shapes—making it more pleasing to her architect's eye. Now it looks like what she saw in Tehran a long time ago: an old red-brick, four-storey building; several newly constructed buildings, stretching up their stony and glassy busts here and there; a dome-like roof with a series of stores guarding the lower part of the building. The juxtaposition is disjointed, reflecting limited architectural taste. It's just.... Not the right time for idle thoughts, she thinks, shaking her head as if trying to get rid of a pesky fly.

Sitting on a tall stool behind the window, with her chin cupped in her left palm and a medium size Tim Horton's cup in her right, Yalda reminds herself of her agenda.

I'd better concentrate on my meeting with Michael, she tells herself.

Yesterday, she had three different phone calls about the same topic, and all the callers—Jimmy, Dan, and Negative Judy—were excited about the news: a new project, which could mean more work.

Yet excitement doesn't leave room for concentration. When she hung up the phone, her thoughts ran in a hundred different directions. She tried to think logically and to follow a single train of thought; she needed to focus on making a decision about her prospective source of income, if not her entire career. Instead, inspired by Dan's reference to the European office, she daydreamed about a potential trip to The Hague, of which she had vivid memories. The career she had always dreamed of, working as a notable architect at a European firm, had always proved to be elusive.

As soon as Yalda understood the underlying message of Judy's call, her heart began to beat faster. It was the pulse of her heart that urged her to make an immediate decision to quit teaching and return to her true vocation. Although she understood the shaky nature of yet another temporary job offer, she couldn't help but grab at any chance of working in her field.

When it comes to choosing between heart and head, Yalda knows that her head always loses the battle.

Her passion for architectural design, fire under ashes, can still be set ablaze with any breeze. Now that the old flame has been rekindled, Yalda feels something warm, yet sad, running under her skin.

She thinks about all the years she couldn't work as an architect, let alone dream to become a legendary one. She snickers to herself.

Once, over a drink with Jimmy, she remembers saying, "I feel like a total failure at my profession of choice." On her first date with him, feeling the pressure of his stare, she had tried to take the lead in the conversation. Yalda also remembers that she felt angry rather than relieved when Jimmy mentioned the role that situation plays in shaping one's life. To justify her vexation, she'd told him that the end result was what counted. Such a statement, though not untrue, was not the real explanation for her feelings. Her failure at work, in fact, was too old to ignite anger. What irked her was what had motivated her to date Jimmy in the first place: he was not an appealing man, but he was a gifted architect.

She knew this the first time she saw his sketches. Admiring them, she interpreted the pang in her heart as a harmless tinge of envy. Yet the feeling continued to creep forward. To lighten the burden of self-blame, Yalda attributed her feelings to her love of architecture. After all, love of beauty can justify jealousy.

Right across the street, she notices the small rampart on the top corner of the red-brick building, and then she casts her eyes down to the honey-coloured hanging lights that framed in the windows of the Starbucks on the ground floor. Not in a mood to linger, Yalda slides her eyes over another old building. This one reminds her of Hasan Abad Square in the early sixties, when it was a beautiful, well-designed square with identical buildings and silver domes.

A ringing cell phone brings her back to the here and now. She removes the lid on her cup to look at the foam and imagine a pattern on it—a trick devised as a low-budget way to quench her thirst for visual pleasure. With no effort or intention, she sees a house in the creamy foam. She blows on it to force the imagined image to vanish before taking a sip.

Not the first time I've built a house and destroyed it, she thinks, as she shifts her focus to the day ahead. In an hour, she would be in the principal's office. In order to guarantee another temp job, she would smile and nod politely as the principal outlined the redundant details about office procedure.

Anticipating the boredom to come, Yalda can't help distracting herself by falling into her memories once again. She sips her coffee and recalls that, years later, she would feel sad whenever she casually passed by Hasan Abad Square. Yalda tended to associate her regret with the thoughtless changes in the square made by mayors with no knowledge of urban design. The bitterness, however, was nostalgic, stemming from the loss of something, someplace, someone, all carved in the grooves of her brain that had deepened since childhood.

On those heavenly days, when she was a little sister pampered by a geeky brother and an eccentric stepsister, Hasan Abad Square was the centre of a small yet safe world. It was the ultimate destination in their meandering through the long hot September afternoons, when "Big Brain" Dadashi and his accomplice "Big Heart" Mati would plan fun trips in the city in an effort to replicate the fun they'd had in the country earlier that summer. The chosen route would usually accommodate a short stop by the office of Agha Jun on tree-lined Amiriyeh Avenue. Yalda would always marvel at the lush green canopies of monstrous plane trees. The "fuel stop"—Dadashi's expression for stopping at his father's office to ask him for money—was an indispensable part of the trip. During the negotiations between "Big Brain" and "Big Fuel Provider" in the office, then considered a manly task, the girls would wait on the sidewalk, discussing what they'd like to spend their money on. An ice cream cone or Alaska ice cream bar was always at the top of the list for Yalda. Depending on how much money they needed for their outing (usually a trip to the movie theatre), various items might appear on their shopping list: a DMC six-strand thread for Mati's cross-stitch hobby; a new foreign brand of matchbox for Yunes's collection; or more pencils, crayons, and chalk for Yalda to draw on the walls and drive Maman Ashi nuts.

Her hand, stretching towards her purse in an urge to grab a pen, stops midway. Instead, she glances at her watch to see how many more minutes she can sit here before heading to the office. She wants to be on time to avoid any sort of small talk with others who, after her long absence, will most likely ask about her job and her son. What can she say about her personal failings? Sticking to this or that gig so that she is always available for a project is not something to be proud of. Rightly or wrongly, she finds it awkward to talk about her son. Thorny questions make her feel like a sea creature, whose body can squirt a sticky, dark liquid. But the liquid, the ink of anger and despair, attacks her own veins rather than protects her.

"No, I'm not going to allow anything to screw up my day," she murmurs.

The wet, shiny pavement of College Street reminds her of

the tender early morning rain. Unlike other early mornings, today she got up right after waking without feeling blue, even though it was grey and bleak outside. Opening the window and feeling the fresh, damp air on her skin, Yalda sensed the presence of spring just around the corner.

Spring is still my main Energizer Bunny, she thinks and smiles to herself.

The image of a silly pink toy rabbit appears for a second, but is quickly replaced with another symbol of spring: Amu (Uncle) Nowruz. The image of a laughing old man who, with his white beard and red cloak, resembles Santa Claus, reminds her of a certain New Year that was not happy. Not for Dadashi, who received his first and last slap from Agha Jun, or for Mati who stayed in bed fighting a cough, or for Little Sis, Yalda, who couldn't find a smile on any of the faces around her.

Ironically, what made that Nowruz so unhappy was the effort to make it great fun. Dadashi was too old for the games they used to play: stealing pastries from the tables arranged by Maman Ashi or mismatching the shoes of important guests. He no longer wanted to pour ground pepper in the coat pockets of Agha Jun's rural guests. These visitors would bring odd presents from the village in the hope of getting a job at the factory of their "distinguished" relative or receiving a "remarkable" reciprocal gift—a gold coin or a couple of brand new bills. Pranks like these turned out to be *démodé*, in Mati's words. Mati had the final authority in determining what was in style and what was *démodé*. That Mati was the only one in "our true family"—in Dadashi's words—who knew French was the grounds for her authority. The fact that Sister Eti's son, Kami, had several tutors, including one for French, didn't matter at all—not because Kami, the same age as Dadashi, was a spoiled only child, but because he belonged to "our false family."

And that year, Mati couldn't plant pansies in the symmetrical garden beds alongside the blue-tiled *howz*. Instead, she had to lie in bed, bored and unable to do anything but count the days until Uncle Nowruz would arrive.

Other than Dadashi, who else could cheer her up? Who else, other than "Big Brain" Dadashi, could come up with a plan good enough to meet with Mati's satisfaction? All masters and magicians, though, have assistants. And who else, other than Little Sis, would get the honour of being an assistant? As the plan began to unfold, though, Yalda began to think of herself as an "accomplice," which sounded weird and suspicious.

Of everything that happened, Yalda can remember only a few images. The first image is of Dadashi grinning at her after she stole Maman Ashi's red robe and gave it to him. Next, she can see herself squatting next to Mati's bed, staring at the eucalyptus-scented vapour dancing softly as it emerged from the heater. Mati was reading a story that was interrupted by her coughing. Then the head and shoulders of a laughing old man with a white beard and a red robe appeared behind the foggy window. And the last image is of Agha Jun stretching out his long arm and slapping Dadashi in the face.

Yalda never forgot this punishment.

Yet the slap was not for the failed prank, which had made Mati scream rather than smile—Agha Jun would not smack his favourite son because of a joke, no matter how troublesome it was. It was clear to everybody, even to Maman Ashi who'd blown the whistle, that the slap, given and taken in silence, was the penalty for disclosing a shameful secret.

As it happened, the secret, a long-forgotten family disgrace, was that Amu, the elder brother of Agha Jun, was kept in the farthest and darkest part of their vast basement after a stroke had disabled him. His carefully hidden presence, almost equal to non-existence, was a topic forbidden to anybody in the household. The only people who ever mentioned it were the ever-changing maids, who often brought it up to ask for a pay raise for their caretaking services. Even Dadashi, who occasionally visited Amu in secret, did not breathe a word about him, possibly because Mati and Yalda were afraid of even thinking about a living creature in the "dungeon," in Mati's words.

It turned out, though, that the creature in the dungeon had nothing to do with vampires, witches, or even jinns.

While Mati was screeching, little Yalda marvelled at the funny elf face in the misty windowpane. At the moment, the shoulders of Dadashi, carrying the made-up Amu Nowruz, were out of sight thanks to his folded knees.

Despite Amu's appealing face and Dadashi's exquisite performance, it was not fun at all.

Years later, when he was Dadash Yunes rather than Dadashi, he confessed that he had been tickling Amu's feet to make him laugh. The confession, or maybe his lighthearted tone, made Yalda feel a shiver of annoyance run down her spine.

How could he have tickled a vulnerable old man to make Mati happy? she'd wondered.

Reading her mind, he expressed regret over tickling the old man's feet, but he maintained that it was the only post-stroke adventure for Amu, who lived a long life until everyone forgot to feed him in the hectic days of Agha Jun's death ceremonies.

She'd had nothing to say to him, so she turned her face away.

Coming back to the present, Yalda thinks to herself that even spring can't accommodate such withered memories.

Changing her posture, she sips the last drops in her cup before leaving the coffee shop. On her way to the office, she tries to focus on the present. But her mind flies to the future when the gate of the past is kept closed.

She'll jolly Michael along during the meeting in order not to kill her chances. Even though she'll feel a bit uneasy when she leaves his room, she anticipates the cleansing of the fresh, late March day that will be waiting for her. After strolling the rain-washed sidewalks and window shopping, she will book her flight to The Hague and call Afi, Ali's sister, to see if there is a chance of staying over at her place. If there is, she'll be able to afford a ticket for Nader and will offer him a free short trip to Europe. That should spark old feelings in his heart. After all, his memories of The Hague cannot all be bitter. When they lived there, he was pampered with double attention and affection, both from a single mother with enough savings and time and from Aunt Afi, who was affectionate with children. Yalda will buy a pot of cat grass and other items for the *haft-sin*, the special table used for Nowruz, and then she'll offer him the ticket as a gift. She will persuade him, in a roundabout way, to consider a new option—living or studying in Europe—before getting enmeshed in a soul-consuming vocation. She will....

She stops at the edge of the sidewalk. Out of the blue, her pot of dreams falls down to the ground as a movie poster showing a gunman catches her eyes. She fails to return the poster vendor's smile.

17.

MY GOODNESS! WHAT A BREATHTAKING VIEW! *Just a vast sea glittering in the ethereal hands of a bright day! It looks like the Caspian Sea, the first sea ever I saw when I was about the same age as my little Nader.*

Ah! Too bad it isn't the Iranian part of the Caspian, but rather the Dutch part of the North Sea that imprints itself on the mind of my Little Bird. This is his first sea. He is standing right in front of me, with his back towards me and his face towards the horizon.

He steps forward half-heartedly, his bare feet sinking into the sand. The waves are rolling and massing and rumbling; they tumble down over his tiny ankles and recede, their sound diminishing. His feet are fixed, but his hands are raised in fear. As the water retreats, my little Nader advances a step or two before he's stopped in his tracks by a new attack.

I call him once, then twice. I notice, though, that my voice is being swallowed by the roar of incoming waves.

BUT THIS IS A DREAM.

Yalda reassures herself as she wakes up and finds herself in Afi's upstairs guest room. To push back a sudden dull back pain, she stretches her stiff body and prepares to get up by reminding herself of the day ahead and her daily tasks. A Sunday after a working Saturday, it is the only free day of a short business stay in The Hague to indulge in a combination of rest and visiting with Afi. Getting out of the unfamiliar bed, it occurs to her that her little son, even when facing an overwhelming monster like the sea, didn't turn his face towards her.

The yellow sticky note on the fridge door implies that Yalda should erase "visiting with Afi" from today's agenda. It reads: *Sorry, must rush to the nursing home to care for the doctor. Make yourself at home and treat yourself to a restful day.*

"Another day of daddy-sitting for poor Afi," Yalda says under her breath.

Looking around the bright, clean kitchen to see how she can make a quick cup of coffee, she admits she has no sympathy for the doctor, the supposedly supportive husband who turned out to be a man with poor heath and dubious wealth. Despite Yalda's cold feelings for him, which may come from his background as a royalist, she respects Afi's decision.

Yet even Yalda has to admit that the doctor has not done anything wrong. In 1993, during Yalda's first visit to The Hague, Afi said that she'd proposed to him to kill two birds with one stone. Years of refugee status, along with chronic loneliness, had led Afi to a point where she only had two options: joining her only brother, Ali, in Saint-Étienne to live under the supremacy of Natalie, her bossy sister-in-law, or finding a husband and provider. A former radical leftist, Afi could not get her head around the idea of hunting for a rich husband, and Yalda had thought that her friend's chances were slim to none regardless.

Thus, during a temporary care-giving job, Afi found a man whose ashen face was marked by old age and heartbreak. The doctor, a panic-stricken former diplomat of an overthrown monarchy, abandoned by his money-sucking wife and children, couldn't help but accept such a decent offer of permanent care.

Yalda recalls her conversation with Afi about her decision to marry the doctor.

"At first, he was hesitant," Afi murmured, trying not to wake little Nader who was asleep on the living room chesterfield.

Settling on the dark walnut chair next to the window, she turned her face to the backyard flowerbed to avoid Yalda's stare.

"What a considerate gentleman!" Yalda snickered, her eyes fixed on the dull brown of the empty chair.

Pulling a Nescafé jar out of the cupboard, she wonders how rude she had appeared to Afi when she had questioned her marriage. Afi, knowing about her hard time in Essen, had offered Yalda help by inviting her and Nader to stay with her and her husband. Instead of appreciating this generosity, Yalda had started criticizing the doctor behind his back for accepting a proposal that no man could resist.

"How stupidly certain I was that I was right!" she mumbles to herself now.

She had expressed her unfavourable view of Afi's decision candidly enough to nettle Afi. Realizing that she had overstepped, Yalda had stopped and tried to behave herself. However, if Afi had been as open as she used to be in the first days of their acquaintance, Yalda would have kept scolding.

She holds the kettle under the tap and remembers her excuse. "Pardon me. I'm so excited to see you after ages that I spoke without thinking." She pauses and turns back to the walnut chair, as if expecting Afi to still be sitting there after all these years.

"Sorry, Afi. I was stupid." This is what she would say to her this time, if the doctor's half-dead body let Afi have a break.

But the apology would be for the stupidity that was a result of her illusions and inexperience, rather than her position on the incompatibility of Afi and the doctor. With eyes on a row of modest pansies next to graceful purple tulips in the bed of flowers behind the window, Yalda reflects on her naïve mindset in those days.

Despite an awkward year staying at her sister's place in Essen—which she had spent in a purgatory state, not knowing what to do—Yalda was still hopeful. She had no doubt that she could survive on her own and raise her little son without any help from anybody. Even though she had no intention of giving Afi a piece of her mind, she couldn't hide her contempt for the way Afi made her living. After all, she was convinced that Afi, who had lived with guerrillas in team houses or in prison, should not have given up her adventurous lifestyle. She should have been as strong and self-confident as those guerrillas who'd been her role models. Even Yalda, who was against any form of violence with all her being, including the armed struggle of the opposition against the Shah, could not shake her impression of the heroic guerillas.

The water gurgles, and Yalda focuses her attention on making coffee. When the heavenly aroma wafts through the kitchen, it occurs to her that reflection on the past is nothing but a pain in the ass. Before going to the fridge for milk, she can't resist the temptation to draw on the misty windowpane. She wonders if she is doing it to have a clear view or to confront the idea of ignoring the past. The first things a foggy windowpane reminds her of are those old days when Mati would encourage her to draw on it instead of flattening her nose against it like their naughty brother.

With hands embracing the hot mug, Yalda pauses in the middle of the room, unsure what to do. The living room, gloomy behind the thick velvet curtains twined with lace, gives her the impression of a tomb. Yalda is surprised that years of living in Holland didn't change Afi's habit of protecting her privacy, "à la mode de chez Iraniens."

What does she have to hide? Yalda thinks. She is sure Afi never appears naked or even half-naked in the living room. Little wonder Afi, raised in a provincial, fanatical family, is faithful to this Eastern style of secrecy. Yet Yalda tends to attribute it to Afi's life in team houses, the secret homes of guerrilla fighters. That such a life was an odd twist of fate rather than one Afi chose doesn't make any difference.

When she pulls back not only the velvet curtain, but also the lace one, Yalda feels a trace of shame. As if the light of day, even a pale day with no sun, reveals that she is condemning Afi in a malicious way. To redeem herself, she considers going to the nursing home to visit with Afi. She had intended to wander the streets, recalling faded memories of being a single mother whose son's hand in hers gave her hope.

"When hesitating between two options, choose the third." The advice of Piruz flashes through her mind. She listened to his advice when she chose to flee abroad rather than to stay married or get divorced. She takes her eyes off the bleak sky and turns towards the room. Now she can see that the room is the same as it was years ago, except for the tenuous touch of age. The old sofa with its luscious cupcake-like cushions catches her eye. Instead of going to *Het Plein* in search of lost time or visiting a terminal patient, she'd rather enjoy her coffee in solitude.

Yet solitude doesn't bring serenity. The doctor, in his heyday, with eyes shining under thick eyebrows, is staring at her. If a guest had the right to change her host's decorations, Yalda would remove this gilded picture frame. "It's not trendy at all to have family photos in a public room," Yalda says to herself, wondering if she's fooling herself or the host. Not a trace, but a wave of shame runs under her skin. Looking down, she mutters, "Sorry, Doctor. I'm not an appreciative guest."

The confession makes her courageous enough to look at the doctor's face again. It's hard to connect this handsome face on the wall to the palliative patient in a bed. It occurs to Yalda that Afi couldn't have fallen in love with the doctor when he was healthy or handsome. When they met, he had already needed care-giving. Sipping her coffee, Yalda thinks that this hypothesis, along with the fact that the doctor no longer had money, refutes the assumption that Afi approached the doctor to take advantage of him. With a sigh of relief, Yalda smiles at his picture. "Otherwise, how could she have taken care of you for all these years?" she asks the doctor staring back at her from the photograph.

Nonetheless, the idea fails to prove that Afi is a saint; rather, it highlights the brutality of destiny. "Well, I can't say more than that, Doctor." Yalda takes her eyes off him and turns to her smiling friend in a thin wooden frame, right below the doctor's, on the bookcase.

The photo is of Afi and Nader. It is familiar, for Yalda has a copy of it among her disorganized pile of papers and pictures that have been constantly relocated over the years. Whenever she happens to see this photo, she tends to focus on little Nader and his frown. This time, though, it is Afi who catches Yalda's eye. For the first time, she notices something in Afi's smile that had been invisible to her. Afi, her arm around Nader's shoulder, is looking at him with deep affection. Yalda knew about Afi's feelings for her little Nader, and about her own longing for a child. From the moment she met them at the airport, Afi showed great interest in Nader, who was reluctant to make friends with strangers. No, what Yalda was blind to was that Afi's affection, love mingled with regret, showed traces of envy as well.

"You should appreciate your child-free life, Afi," Yalda grumbles, closing her eyes to little Nader.

Taking a big gulp of her lukewarm coffee, she recalls how Afi's expression changed when she noticed Nader was not with her on this second trip to The Hague. On the way from the airport to the house, after trying to decide on the right excuse to explain his absence, Yalda ended up saying, "Afi, dear, my son is not a predictable boy."

A flood of reproach, coming from Afi, made Yalda change her mind about telling her friend the truth.

"But I wanted to tell you, Afi, how harrowing this hidden wound is," Yalda whispers to the photograph. Blinking, she lets her teardrops fall, feeling glad that Afi is not here to see her.

18.

"YOU CALLED ME, BIRDIE, DIDN'T YOU?" She utters the words loudly enough to be heard by both her ears and the bird's. The street, shining after the early morning drizzle, is reserved for early birds. Standing still on the sidewalk, Yalda waits for a response.

She wonders if it might be a vireo. The bird doesn't resume its warble. It would be useless to repeat the question. Yalda is sure it's around, perching on a topmost twig or a roof edge, or squatting somewhere in the hedge. She's heard the song, distinctive among the intermittent sparrow chirps, robin chirrups, and cardinal cheeps. She is also positive that she can't make the bird call to her again. For a while, she gives up on her hearing and turns to her sight and smell. Right in front of her, the narrowing view of the street with rows of blooming crab apple trees along each side looks like a heavenly corridor. Greedy for the sweet scent of May, she inhales the fresh air and keeps walking to the point where the two parallel lines might meet.

No, she won't repeat her question. And the bird may not sing again. Yet it was the question that made her get out of the bed, pass the closed door, and leave home for a walk in the early Sunday morning. Otherwise, how could she overcome the acute back pain after a six-day work week, hunching over the drafting table. It was the question that made her resilient not only against pain, but also against the depression that was part of her morning routine since that horrible Thursday of last October.

Of all her dreams last night, she can't remember anything other than the familiar question repeating itself, detached from any images or thoughts. With no bird song, or even a dream of her Little Bird, the question doesn't make much sense. Nonetheless, it was uttered with her own voice, a message coming from nowhere, or an intrusive signal from the off-duty part of her brain to the on-duty part.

Here and now, awake and away from home, it makes sense, though. If the bird hadn't called out to her, she would have been stuck in front of the door of Nader's room. Its call was a buffer against the disappointment of seeing that door closed to her, Nader's code for "incommunicado." This morning, she lingered for a moment at the door, recalling Nader's last word to her: when she had asked him to accompany her to The Hague, his response had been, simply, "No." The frustration of this latest failure was overwhelming enough to knock her down. But the question, the bird's early morning call to her, began to beat in her mind and enabled her to pass by the door and run to the bathroom, where she washed her face with water.

Out on the street, the delicate touch of a May breeze rouses her, helping her to ignore the fresh wound of a Nader who is not little anymore. She pauses and closes her eyes to let her skin be caressed. A flash of fantasy makes her feel like she is being touched by the soft tips of her Nader's fingers. The pleasure may soon be replaced by a lurking agony—it is almost the anniversary of the loss of her Nader, which cannot be ignored.

But Yalda has learned how to deal with this particular sorrow over the years. After forty days madly mourning for her Nader, she stopped grieving his loss. With no tears in her eyes, no cry in her throat, no energy in her body, she had found a devastating hollow inside herself that threatened not only her being, but also the memory of her Nader.

Then, out of the blue, a stranger, a girl in blue jeans and a long-sleeved men's shirt, had appeared at the threshold of her room, claiming she had a message from Nader Yeganeh.

"You don't look like a jinn," she said with a hoarse voice hardly above a whisper.

"My name is Afi," she said, with a clear and pure tone. "My brother, Ali, was in the cell with your Nader for his last days."

This was how Afi had entered her life, on a hot sunny day. Unlike her *hamzad*, Afi was calm, detached, yet patient enough to ignore Yalda's melancholic behaviour and keep coming to visit her for a couple of months. She disappeared when Yalda had gotten over her bereavement.

It was Afi who helped her fill the hollow inside herself caused by the absence of her Nader. Not that Afi had any plan or method. During her short, unexpected visits, Afi, cautious not to give any information that might cause problems, would talk only about herself, a subject that, at the time, made Yalda's eyes glaze over. Born in a small northern town, she found herself in a team house of leftist guerrillas in Tehran simply by following her older brother, who in turn was following his friends. Her brother, like Yalda's Nader, survived the Shah's jail and got caught in the new regime's trap. Years later, Afi described how she fell in love with Nader, a man she had never met. Her brother, who had been his cellmate, talked about and praised him often, and Afi felt like she knew him well. This part of the story, which back then had struck Yalda as a childish love story of a naïve provincial girl, later helped her to develop the capacity for a long-distance relationship with a partner beneath the ground.

Stopping for a minute to take a deep breath, Yalda considers how a relationship with a dead beloved, despite its dark moments, has its benefits. First among them is that such a love, unlike a love with a living man, can last as long as she likes. There is another advantage, though, that attracts her the most: it is accessible. Although ashamed about this selfish attitude,

Yalda can't give up the advantage of her Nader. Awake or asleep, she always calls upon him whenever she misses him: in her lonely, desperate moments; in fear and anger; even in joy and pleasure. She's been with her Nader not only in the loneliness of her bed, but also in the presence of another partner.

"Or maybe you come to me, wanted or unwanted, my Nader," she wonders with a faint smile on her face.

With arms wide open, she steps towards the convergence point, where the two sides of the street appear to come together. Although the sides will never meet, the fallacious point at the end of the street will lead her to the right spot, where she will find a weeping willow at the entrance to a ravine on the corner.

"Don't we always rendezvous under a willow?" she asks, walking more quickly to feel the light wind beneath her arms.

The May breeze had played with Yalda's dark free-flowing hair as she sat on a bench under a young willow in Niavaran Park. She was about to have her first date with her first boyfriend. In the short phone conversation with Nader, a fine arts student who taught painting part-time in a private school, she had suggested this park as the right place for a rendezvous. Later on, when Nader was no longer a stranger but her Nader, she disclosed to him that Niavaran Park, the city's newest park in the city's far north end, came to mind as the safest place from the reach of Dadash Yunes, who was living and working in a small town.

"So, little girl, are you afraid of being caught by your older brother even when he is far from Tehran?" Nader laughed lightheartedly.

"First of all, I'm seventeen, not a little girl, but I'll always be a little sister to him..."

"And second of all?" he interrupted her, still laughing.

"Second? I won't say anything unless you stop laughing at me." She frowned and waited for him to change her expression with a stealthy kiss.

"And second of all, my Nader, Dadash Yunes can come to Tehran any time to visit me without notice. Who else does he have in Tehran, other than a parentless little sister who doesn't give a damn about the advice of relatives?"

"You'd better not be a bad girl, sweetie," her Nader murmured, trying to braid a few strands of her hair with a willow twig that was hanging down over her shoulder.

The shadow of a passing cloud slides over the momentarily vivid image of the past and leaves no trace of it behind. Having stopped for a minute to let her tired arms fall to her sides, Yalda blinks to acknowledge that the image is gone. Now, instead of the point of convergence, she sees the intersection where roads and lines meet and depart. She keeps walking, her pace steady, her eyes sliding past the trees on each side of her. She lets her mind return to the past.

As the May breeze played with the light green, free-flowing hair of the willow, Yalda sat on their bench underneath it, awaiting her Nader with great excitement. She was going to celebrate the good news by having a romantic night with him. He had told her on the phone that he had asked her brother for his approval, and Dadash Yunes had given it. In the two years since they started dating, both of them, in different ways, had been worried about Dadash Yunes finding out about their relationship. That his little sister was dating a man she wasn't engaged to would not sit well with his fixed mindset.

Yalda dreamed of living with her Nader under one roof, but he was reluctant to take that step before marriage, and the more she persisted the more hesitant he became. "You're reading all that junk revolutionary stuff, but you don't have the guts to ignore these stupid conventions," Yalda scoffed.

"I'm going to be an artist, not a politician. I read revolutionary literature just to know what's happening in our world." Her Nader blushed with anger. "This aside, I love you enough to want to make the right decision."

"Is it wrong to be together, my Nader?" she asked in a loving voice.

"You may rebel against tradition, but I can hardly believe you can ignore your brother's feelings."

"My Dadashi is not going to hurt his little sis," she stated with conviction.

"We're not going to hurt him either, Yalda."

She was sure that her Nader must have applied some kind of diplomacy in handling her family, by promising to tie the knot soon. In any case, she'd held her breath as she waited for her Nader to appear on the narrow path in front of her.

"But the road remained vacant, my Nader," Yalda says under her breath and stops for a minute to sigh deeply.

He didn't show up until the following year, when some angry mobs stormed the Shah's prisons.

Closing her eyes, Yalda tries to remember her Nader's face, but it refuses to appear and brighten her mind's eye. She looks up to the sky and sees the sun, behind dense clouds, is barely giving any light. She keeps going towards the three-way intersection and continues her inner conversation with him.

"Sitting on our bench until the daylight disappeared, I thought of so many horrible things. But I never considered that you had been arrested by SAVAK for carrying forbidden books in your bag," she says out loud with a bitter smile.

Seven days of wandering around the city, searching restlessly for the trace of a missing man; seven nights rolling over in bed feeling butterflies in her belly, bruises under her skin, and a disturbance in her head.

"Yet we both survived that first tragedy, my Nader," she murmurs, "not knowing another one was on its way."

Feeling the gloom of an overcast sky, she takes brisk steps and decides to avoid reliving the second tragedy by interrupting her inner talk with her Nader. She notices that the birds have fallen silent. She can tell that a second rainfall is coming soon and that she will get wet. Reaching the intersection, she turns left, down into the ravine.

Along a short stretch of a sloped path, the tree appears in the rain. Letting the drops run over her face, she smiles and whispers:

"Hey, willow, fellow
Why are you weeping? My love is arising
Oh, willow, fellow
Birdie is coming. Stop crying!"

19.

BEFORE TURNING THE KNOB, SHE LEANS her forehead against the wooden door with the devotional feeling of a pilgrim who has reached a shrine. Touching wood makes her feel restful. Instead of prayer, she heaves a long sigh. Another no-overtime Saturday work day is done and she feels satisfied rather than tired or pissed off as she usually does. When it comes to her job the glass is definitely not full, or even half full. She's simply watching the glasses of others.

Yalda wonders if her son is home. She feels her heart rate pick up. Through all the days of this restless month of June, glistening threads of hope have crossed along the surface of the hidden sea of her anger and despair, and have finally appeared in her consciousness.

When she opens the door, she doesn't see the familiar sign of his presence: his bulky boots right in the middle of the hallway. The carelessly removed shoes, now a promising sign, used to drive her mad and make her curse under her breath as she put, sometimes threw, them in the closet. The rough boots, an awkward reminder of his "rough and tough" dream job, are now simple evidence of his presence.

Still, he may be home but asleep, she thinks, perhaps without taking his boots off.

Putting the takeout box on the kitchen counter, she glances towards his room and notices that the door is half open.

This may mean a change, she thinks. Her hands busy transferring food into dishes, Yalda counts off the months by clattering her teeth, stopping at eight. Well, after eight months of encountering a closed door, it's no wonder that she thinks a half-open door is a good sign.

Passing by the door and peeping into his room, she finds his bed empty. Yalda forces herself to ignore the messy room, reminding herself that she's picked her battles.

"His damn rotating shift work schedule has ruined my appetite," she mumbles as she puts the food in the fridge, "and my plan, too."

Driven by a desire for revenge rather than a sudden craving for alcohol, she grabs the bottle of Martini Rosso that she got from the duty free store in Rotterdam. She smiles nervously when she finds some dried white mulberries in her beloved turquoise ceramic bowl. Despite Nader's absence, she's going to have her exclusive Iran news fest.

C'est la vie, she thinks, turning her eyes away from the table that was supposed to be set for him. After putting her laptop, her martini, and the bowl of mulberries on the side table, she collapses into her rocker.

From her vantage point, the metal rim of the balcony glass balustrade separates a sky deepening with twilight hues from a panel compacted with curves of trees and diagonals of buildings. The glass of the panel is spotted with rain and handprints, and she feels guilty for not keeping it sparkling clean. Above the rim, the sunset scene with its cosmic perfection makes her sad. It reminds her of her enduring imperfection, her stale incompleteness. A deep desire for company bursts through her, and she feels heat rise in her body.

"I don't even have the jinn to keep me company at this time of day," she says to herself, thinking about the remaining hours of daylight and the degree of her sanity.

When she turns her eyes towards the side table, she notices two glasses on it. Why did she bring two glasses? She knows the second glass wasn't for Nader, or for the jinn.

"And the guy from Mars is not landing at my place either," she assures herself with a laugh.

Not giving up on finding company, she sits her cheap IKEA mirror on a chair in front of hers. Raising her glass with a smile, she gazes at herself.

"Let's toast each other's good company, my dear." Yalda puts the glass to her lips without taking her eyes off the image. "And toast to a failed plan as well."

She sips her drink and resumes her conversation. "Not a real plan, though. Just a kind of hope that looked like a speck of glitter at first, then stretched itself out, filling the space between your cells."

What she felt was a kind of balloon-like anticipation, but she didn't really expect it to work out.

"Well, I couldn't help it, you know," she continues. "It started with the torrent of news about the presidential election scam in Iran. I don't remember exactly when Nader first dropped by my room to listen to the news or watch the video clips."

Yalda puts a couple of mulberries in her mouth and gives herself time to think. Since the beginning of the month, she has been spending hours browsing the internet for the latest news about an ongoing series of mass protests against electoral fraud. She didn't have much interest or time to join solidarity events and rallies organized by Iranian community groups in the city, so she contented herself with online news.

"But that night, at midnight, I was replaying like mad the video clip showing Neda bloom and die on the hot asphalt of a Tehran street. Then Nader appeared over my shoulder and offered me a single tissue."

She takes a large gulp of her drink, recalling that, sobbing, she had said nothing. After a second, he went back to his room as quietly as he'd come. That night, unable to pull herself together, she didn't notice what Nader had done. The next day though, opening up her eyes to the morning light, she remembered it and found a bit of hope deep inside her.

"I wonder if the horrible things happening over there could rebuild the burnt bridge between Nader and me," she says, looking into the mirror and seeing the desperate desire sparkling in her eyes.

And desire, with or without hope, will grow, Yalda reminds herself.

"Don't deny what you want!" she says to herself in the mirror, her voice hoarse with emotion. "I'm telling you, it's okay for you to want such brutal atrocities to open your son's eyes! You should know, though, that if you stretch your desire too much, it'll snap and hurt you, just like an elastic band."

She notices the eyes in the mirror are now shining with tears. Yalda fills the other glass and starts drinking from it. As alcohol washes down the lump in her throat, she blames herself for her obsession with Nader's plans, reminding herself that numerous youths in Iran are under attack. But her guilt vanishes as quickly as a puff of smoke and is replaced by rationalizing.

"I read your mind, poor mother," she says, nodding at her reflection. "It makes sense for you to want to keep your son away from both sides of the conflict. Who fights crimes and how is none of your business…"

A wave of doubt, surging through her body, interrupts her. She grabs some mulberries to soothe the bitter taste in her mouth. Avoiding eye contact with herself in the mirror, she hears a string of words in her head: law, order, obedience, public safety, prevention, protection….

"Yes, protection, protection, protection!" She jumps back into her conversation with herself, her tone suddenly heavy with sadness. "This word is always at the forefront for foolish moms like me."

Yalda is exhausted, and her conversation with herself dies down. She listens to her inner wisdom caution against binge drinking, and refrains from refilling the glass. She brings out her laptop and leans back in her chair, still hoping that Nader will come back home before she goes to bed and has a nightmare. Browsing the internet in search of recent reports on the crackdown and chaos, she lands on a YouTube video of young demonstrators throwing stones at cops, who are chasing them with batons and tear gas.

She pauses it. Over there, she knows, her son could have been a victim of police violence.

"If you carry a gun, dear, the most you could be is a good bad guy," she moans under her breath.

She hears two axioms in her head:

"*Only a naïve idealist tries to escape reality.*"

"*To beat evil, you need an iron fist, not a velvet hand.*"

To dodge the attack, Yalda turns off the laptop and closes her eyes, trying to escape from the here and now. Willing herself to stay awake in the darkness, she makes a tunnel in her mind and steps into it, returning to her memories.

Little Sis was left alone on the sidewalk by her big brother who'd gone to Agha Jun's office to ask for an "extra bonus." It was hard to remember if she was in grade one or if it was earlier. It was the time when Mati was sick in bed, coughing and moaning and cursing herself for catching a cold. Not a common cold, as Dadashi explained on the way home from school. That sort of "important ailment" demanded special attention, Big Brain had concluded. The two sympathetic siblings wanted to express their love with an extraordinary gift, a gesture that would not be possible without negotiating with the mighty money-maker. Waiting for Dadashi by a plane tree, she was amused by her surroundings: yellowish leaves hanging, trembling in the chilly October wind, passersby going in different directions, and cars speeding by in the street. A bulky beggar limped along the row of stores on crutches, followed by a skinny stray dog wagging behind him quietly. A raw-boned police officer walked up and down the sidewalk; whichever direction he went, the beggar and his dog chose the opposite way. Later she asked her big brother why.

"The officer has a baton," he said.

"What is a baton, Dadashi?"

"A baton? Well, it's the devil's bloody little finger."

Although little Yalda likely dreamed of the devil's bloody finger that night, the story of the devil and his finger was forgotten for a long, long time.

She didn't remember it until the horrible day when she came back from the morgue.

Piruz, frightened of seeing the corpse, had stayed in the car and then asked, "How was it?"

Still feeling woozy, she heard him repeating the question.

"How the heck was it?"

Bang, Bang, Bang!

"For the devil's sake, open your mouth, Yalda! What did you see over there?"

"The devil's bloody little finger on his head." This crawled out of her memory, rather than her mouth.

"A hole in his head?" Piruz asked in a frightened, deep-throated voice.

No! What she'd seen in the callous light of that December day in 1991 was not a hole in a head—just three thin lines over the head of a corpse that hardly reminded her of her beloved Dadashi.

A couple of days ago, she saw a hole in a head—in the video clip she found that disturbing midnight when she frenetically surfed the virtual world. It captured the aftermath of a night attack on a university dorm. She watched it over and over again that night, but has not found it again since.

A tsunami of words and images flowed out from a land that was bleeding under the devil's deadly paws; and among numerous faces, among the voluminous cries, among the many shocking scenes, it was this image that stuck in her mind for good.

Narrow, intersecting corridors, constantly shaking, were lit by the dirty yellow of trembling ceiling lights and haunted by shadowy figures running around frantically. In the chaotic merging and re-emerging of horrifying colours and terror-stricken sounds, and amidst the tangle of legs and arms dragging the victim—a Jesus-like face with a blank look and a deep, dark red hole in the head.

AND IT WAS NOT A DREAM.

Yalda opens her wet eyes to gaze into the dark mirror set in front of her.

20.

AS USUAL, THE PAIN HITS HER WITH NO NOTICE, right beneath her left shoulder blade, which is stiff after several hours of slouching over a desk. Whether it will sprawl around like an ink stain spreading over a sheet of paper, or keep condensing within itself, it is a reminder to put her pencil down and take a break.

But what am I supposed to do other than work? she thinks.

Working in her own field gives her solace and pleasure, particularly while the landscape beyond her desk is so gloomy. To mitigate the pain, Yalda counts her immediate blessings: a project, an easy pre-charrette period, a bright summer Saturday, and an empty office that she can imagine is all hers.

To alleviate the pain and boost her imagination, she takes a deep breath and leaves her desk to grab some water. "I'll need to put in more effort if I want to pretend this office is mine," she says to herself.

Visualizing the gait of the big boss, who she has only seen two or three times, she decides it's not authoritative enough. Instead, she makes up her mind to imitate Michael's walking style, which would give anybody the impression that he thinks he's the boss. When she passes by his desk, she notices a family picture dangling from a clip rail. Beside his large wife and behind his chubby twins, the pint-sized Michael looks like a modest twig. Recalling his sweet, obedient tone while talking to his wife over the phone, Yalda can't help but titter.

"Enjoy your time in Dubai, my dear long-distance boss, not far from the massive crown," she says aloud.

In the kitchen, more like the lady of the house than a boss, she checks to see if everything is clean and tidy. No surprise. Michael's absence means a mess in the kitchen: mugs and cups and greasy containers left unwashed in the sink, crumbs and stains on the countertops, unhung towels, and a full trash can. Negative Judy's icy voice echoes in her head. "A messy kitchen is a living kitchen, a kitchen that is alive."

Yalda avoids thinking of the reason why she finds Judy's voice irksome. She wonders if such a "kitchuation" legitimizes Michael's bossiness. She cleans the counter, ignoring the dishes in the sink, and grabs a water bottle from the fridge.

Making herself at home on the only leather lounge chair, she reaches into her Fendi leather bucket bag for a painkiller, but can't locate it without pulling things out one by one. "Damn fashion for turning a bag into a bucket," she mumbles.

She has to blame herself for accepting it as a gift from Afi though it's not to her taste.

It occurs to her that making herself busy searching—setting each item in her lap and then returning it all to the bag—would be an acceptable alternative to her favourite time-killing method, doodling, when she is on a break. It reminds her, though, of the purse-digging habit of her least favourite sister, Eti, and of Maman Ashi's obsessive practice of taking things in and out of her antique wooden treasure chest.

No time for the dead, least-loved or best-loved, she tells herself.

With delicate care, Yalda arranges the contents of her bag in her lap: nail cutter, nail file, tweezers, lipstick, rarely-used makeup, comb, hair ties, mirror, wallet, key chain, notebook, pen and pencils, Advil, and cell phone. She is interrupted by a stab of pain. She takes the painkiller and then gulps half the bottle of water down afterwards. She no longer has any interest in arranging things, so she goes back to thinking about having her own office. She finds the idea of possession kind of "tacky," as Piruz used to say about their office in Tehran. He thought it was tasteless and showy, with lots of obligations. For a moment, just a moment, she feels the same.

Nonetheless, this office—with no bothersome people or sounds—is appealing to her and gives her the impression of a temporary haven.

This office, even though it belongs to others, is a refuge for her, while out there, in the city, she never sees familiar faces in the crowd. And home? It feels awkward to be home, where a young man, supposedly her son, wears a weird mask with no eyes, no ears, no mouth.

Yalda dumps everything back into the bag other than her cell phone. An urge to be connected spurs her to turn it on, though she doesn't anticipate any calls. But there is a missed one.

"Oh, no! Again, Nandita! Another call about Asuntha?" she grumbles. She is not in the mood to call anyone back. But, feeling ashamed for not returning Nandita's call, she looks for a good excuse.

"Look, Nandita. I got your message. That's too bad. It's hard to know what to say," she says under her breath, picturing Nandita's dark brown eyes full of questions.

The message, the latest news about Asuntha, is the sort of thing that makes her feel dumb. Yalda replays Nandita's voice in her head, reviewing what has happened to Asuntha. She was harassed, injured, taken to the hospital, released, and is now stuck in bed like a stone in concrete. Yalda remembers Nandita's story about the collusion of an evil sister-in-law and a betraying demon. She imagines Nandita scratching her cheeks.

"My goodness! Couldn't I have some happy people around me?" she murmurs.

Looking for something to brighten her mood, she scrolls up and down her list of contacts. She skips Dan lest she be tempted to call him, and lands with some hesitation on Jimmy. In her mind's eye, Yalda sees his face; he has clean-cut features, but his odd stare overshadows his beauty. She recalls the vague smile lurking at the corner of his lips when she'd said, "We're not a good fit, Jimmy." To avoid calling him accidentally, she scrolls further down, remembering his words: "Not a marriage proposal; a sex proposal." She'd smiled coldly in response and told him he was disgusting.

It occurs to her now that perhaps she had never been fair to him. Setting aside his obnoxious obsession, Yalda had enjoyed his company, particularly in those rare moments when he was focused on art and architecture. She had not been honest with him, either.

"What would you like to see in me, Yalda?" Jimmy had asked her, using a lower-pitched voice and sliding his hand over the table towards hers.

Her response had been nothing but a low hum of chagrin. How could she tell him about her big expectations? The man she'd wanted to see in front of her was a guy with Jimmy's artistic sense, Dan's looks, Marc's compatibility, Piruz's self-determination, and her Nader's noble spirit, all in one package. She would have been ready to minimize her ideals, though, and even ignore the wide age gap, if only Jimmy had not been a womanizer.

"Jimmy, I'm sorry that real happiness has been out of reach for you," she says, feeling sudden sympathy for him. After all, he was just a guy who was looking for sex with no strings attached.

When she lands on Nader's name, she feels the pain moving and expanding beneath her breast. When she thinks about Nader, what appears in front of her mind's eye is the figure of a man tucked up in the fetal position: no face, no familiarity. She sits up straight and raises her chest to lessen the pain. Indifferent to her attempts, it tightens around her torso like a stiff corset. Yalda gets up, her phone in her hand, and paces back and forth.

"Damn pain, you're not going to scare me," she groans,

forcing herself to ignore it by focusing on Nader.

She has to admit that the more she thinks about her son, the less she seems to understand him. Just a couple of weeks ago, at the peak of the chaos in Tehran, he poked his head out of his stone shell of indifference and gave Yalda a sort of faint hope. It didn't last long, though.

It was nothing more than a little blink of light on the dull sea of dense clouds, she thinks.

He has shut her out again, but she's not sure if he's trying to escape her snooping or if he's gone back to his habitual mood.

"I can keep pounding on the door," she says aloud, "but I know I cannot break it down."

In a surge of helplessness, she scrolls down to Piruz and stops walking for a moment. Without a doubt, she is not going to call him after years of no communication and no news. She doesn't want to swallow her pride and appeal to him. And she knows there is nothing he could do to help her, even if he wanted to.

She walks towards the window. In the light creeping through the blinds, she pictures Piruz as he was when he was young. Through the eyes of the admiring young architecture student that she once was, she can see the profile of a man in his thirties, one of two owners of a small firm.

It's hard to imagine what he would look like now, in his late fifties, she says to herself.

Her brain, not listening to her, keeps conjuring images of Piruz from the office in its early days—without Lady Liaison, who came later as a secretary and became the partner's wife—when it was an intimate studio run by newly-graduated owners and full of student trainees like herself. At that time its wide window, which still had a traditional woven straw shade, let the light through.

The window overlooking the street was her favourite spot to take a short break from the drafting table. The street was not just a busy, noisy main street close to the university campus; it was also a privileged location, at the centre of the revolution that was taking shape, and it bulged with more and more protesters. From the corner window, Yalda would observe the demonstrations below and daydream about her Nader's anticipated release from jail. She would also cast furtive glances at Piruz, who was an enigma to her.

"For me you're still a knot, Piruz," she says, letting out a long sigh. "Without your old charm, though."

Those days, when she was young and naïve, Piruz gave her a kind of cinematic impression—there was something, not in his face or physique, but in his manner, that reminded her of Paul Newman as the tough guy in *The Long, Hot Summer*.

"What the hell are you watching down there so eagerly?" Piruz would ask her with implicit disdain.

"You don't hear their cry for revolution? Things are going to change soon."

"Ah! I know those stupid huddled masses are turning everything upside down."

"Do you think all these people in the street are idiots who don't know what they want?"

"Look, Yalda, you're too young to realize that people are herd animals...."

"What's happening outside this office is not architecture, Piruz. The real life of society does not have the beauty and order of a magnificently designed building."

"What a tactful employee I have! You're right, though. Revolution is not my specialty; it's my nightmare. I'm going to put it out of my mind by going to an expensive restaurant this evening. Would you like to come with me? To celebrate the impending release of your boyfriend from prison?"

Yalda walks around the room again, trying to remember more examples of Piruz's charm. Her other boss, Piruz's business partner, would call these the "Wonders of Piruz."

"You remember, Piruz, I was not the only person who couldn't predict your reactions," she says aloud, still staring at his old phone number. "Under those damned wartime conditions, you wouldn't allow me to take my Little Bird with me back to Tehran. Even with your strong feelings about fundamentalism and fanaticism, you took advantage of the terrible circumstances. Yes, you did what a fanatic male parent would do. But when I took our son to Europe with no return ticket, you made zero effort to assert your Islamic male parental rights. By then, you'd stopped bothering. You hardly kept in touch with our son, only calling him now and then, or sending him a postcard...."

Noticing her rapid heartbeat and hasty steps, she stops and reminds herself of the other side of the coin. No matter her reasons, she'd deprived him of his son. And what did he do? Among all options, he chose his favourite Taoist tactic: doing nothing. Why didn't he take some action? Was he trying to get revenge on his disobedient wife? Or to punish his innocent kid? Or just to protect himself from having to take any responsibility?

"Maybe now you're the super happy man I always wanted, Piruz," she murmurs, "far from the mess I'm sinking in, safe and sound in your orchard haven."

Tired of dealing with an old knotted thread, Yalda collapses into the lounge chair and closes her eyes for a moment, trying to imagine a magic tool that could cut her loose from her tangled relationships, old and new. Nothing appears other than red dots behind her closed eyes. The pain in her back has finally left her alone. Getting ready to go back to work, she takes a deep breath. Before putting the cell phone in her bag, she remembers Nandita's call and decides to listen to her new "messtory": *"Hello, ex-teacher, you are there? No? Long time, no call, Mrs. Teacher. You forget Nandita? No? Asuntha? Rima? Teacher, I told you Asuntha story. No call from you. Now, Mrs. Teacher, I tell you Rima story. Rima son missing, Teacher, his Uncle say he is jail, not Canada jail, Teacher. You understand, no? Good night, Teacher!"*

21.

WITH HER BACK TOWARDS THE SUN and the lake, Yalda takes her sunglasses out of her purse and spreads the straw beach mat on the sand. The old mat, a second-hand gift from her first landlady in Toronto, is still in decent shape. It was left folded up for ages; Nader hadn't shown any interest in a beach outing in years. During their outings to Guildwood—a period that now feels like a faded dream—it was unfolded but never used, for Nader always preferred to perch on a stone.

She looks at her watch. It's half past six. When she got behind the wheel, it was almost dawn. With no destination in mind, she left it to her metallic silver horse to take her away from home once again. This time, it wasn't because she was trying to give Nader space or to occupy herself during a day off, but because she wanted to flee from herself. She wanted to remove herself from a situation where she was tempted to disrespect her son's right to privacy.

She assumed she would find herself at Guildwood. A lakeside park, like Cherry Beach, particularly on a summer Sunday, is not her type of place by any means. In fact, the groups of picnickers bother her; they distract her from feeling in touch with nature. Nonetheless, Yalda is here, not at Guildwood. Maybe her fear of being alone on a remote beach was stronger than the appeal of its serenity. Or perhaps the idea of going out there without Nader was disturbing.

She turns towards the horizon. She's decided to ignore the

lake and to focus on the sun; it's as though they are having a private meeting. She is also careful not to look at the face of the sun before the right time. She feels as though the splendour of the sun at this time of the morning demands something special, a sort of solo ritual—civilized, easy to do, and tailored to her needs. After all, she may have a drop of Mithraic blood in her veins. She takes off her sandals and sits on the mat in a meditation posture: back straight, legs crossed, hands on knees, but with her purse on her lap signalling her attachment to inconsequential belongings. With no intention to watch her breath and with no white wall in front of her to stare at, she keeps her head up and faces the sun.

Quietly, she begins to chant: "Not because you're the lord of the earthians, or the master of life, but because you're the illuminator, I'm begging you to eliminate this damn dark dot." She pauses to swallow her saliva. "I don't mean the suspicion in his mind, but the questioning inside me. Please help me not get caught in the trap of motherly prying. He's testing me by leaving his mail and papers in a certain pattern to see whether or not I touch them—as if I've never seen any detective movies in my life. O Beautiful Lord, Beautiful Mithra! Don't I have the right to know what my son is doing with his soul?" She pauses again to collect herself. "He's lost his trust in me, if he ever had any at all. He never believed I didn't open that letter intentionally. Well, I didn't. But now I feel a strong urge to open this new envelope. As soon as I saw it in his mail, my heart started to beat hard. I bet it's about his application. He didn't open it yesterday, though. Instead he left it on his desk, beside the others. This kind of organization is not his habit. To be honest, this morning when I noticed he was not home yet, I was about to yield to the temptation of examining the envelope and opening it." She smiles nervously.

The sweet face of the sun starts shaking and vibrating. Yalda, mesmerized by the rounded ripples and twinkling colours, feels a sort of epiphany: a pebble dropped in still water, a silent

splash, and no end to the widening circles.
But who dropped the pebble? And when did it happen?
She takes her wet eyes off the sun, puts on her sunglasses, and lies down on her back with the purse on her tummy and her palms on the warm sand. The gentle breeze, carrying the smell of water, sweeps over her body and takes her mind back to the past.

Ali could be a good role model for my baby, she had thought after seeing him sitting on the steps of the Place de l'Hôtel de Ville, elbows on knees, with little Nader's school bag between his legs and a cigarette between his fingers. He was watching Nader wobble on a new skateboard, a birthday gift. Yes, he was certainly becoming a father figure for her son. When Yalda didn't know how to manage attending *l'école,* working at the lingerie store, and taking care of Nader—in his first year of school in Saint-Étienne—Ali appeared. He was like an angel who had come down from heaven to babysit for her. It was hard to ignore such a miraculous offer. He'd assured her that it wouldn't be a hassle for him. He ran a restaurant with Natalie, and being self-employed gave him flexibility. Plus, he enjoyed spending time with a boy who was the son of a dear friend and had the name of another dear friend. When he'd uttered "dear friend," Yalda had noticed his face flush. The blush was living proof of what his sister, Afi, had already told her during her visit to The Hague: Ali was in love with Yalda. At the time, Yalda had interpreted it as a family trait, something both sister and brother had in common: falling in love with someone they had never met. Perhaps this tendency was due to a sort of Eastern romanticism of their generation, which had its hands in harsh reality and its head in idealistic illusions. Afi's love for her Nader, which had arisen from her brother's description of his prison-mate, seemed to Yalda like the fantasy of a young provincial woman whose contact with men had been limited to almost nothing. Ali's love for his adored friend's girlfriend was the other side of the coin.

After all, Ali, although his sister saw him as very learned and mature, was, in fact, a provincial young man whose experience with women could hardly be more than a couple of visits to Shahr-e Now (New City), the well-known whorehouse in the south of Tehran. It was no wonder that such a man would allow Natalie to have the upper hand.

"How come you're smoking while babysitting, Ali?" Yalda said smiling, patting him on the shoulder and sitting beside him on the step.

Ali, preoccupied with his thoughts, didn't welcome her the way he used to. He smiled faintly, though, before collecting himself. "Hey, you're early today!"

She shook her head no, watching her little Nader with glowing affection. "I just ran all the way," she said. "Little Bird, Mom is here! Come give me a kiss!" With no response from little Nader, who was trying to control the skateboard, Yalda turned towards Ali. "I can never thank you enough, Ali."

"Don't mention it, please!" he said with a husky voice.

"Was my Little Bird a good boy today?" she asked, wondering why he hadn't yet told her what they had been up to that afternoon.

"Oh, yeah! He was a bit grumpy, but he had his sandwich and orange juice. He did his homework, too."

"He didn't get on Natalie's nerves, did he?" she asked, a little worried.

"Well, you know, Yalda," his voice fell to a deep whisper, "it seems that Natalie has no desire to get along with this little boy."

"He's not naughty, just stubborn, just...." She stopped, not recognizing her own voice.

"Not his fault at all. Kids can always tell who's a friend and who's a foe...."

He sounded sad and guilty, Yalda remembers. His words were disturbing, and she tried to block them out, but at the same time she instinctively inclined her shoulder towards his. She knew she should not trust her instincts, though. Ali, who was unable to fight back against his demanding partner, could not be a support for her or for her son.

The clamour of children nearby interrupts her thoughts. Opening her eyes, she turns in the direction of the sound, and pushes her glasses up onto her forehead to look around. The beach is filling up with people who seem to be here for anything but swimming. A Frisbee flies through the air; Yalda follows its arc and then shuts her eyes again after it lands on the ground.

Suddenly, she is back in the past again. A shiny yellow Frisbee! Not the right toy for a two-year-old toddler, Yalda thought. Piruz looked more excited than his son, and assured her it would be fun to try it in the park that afternoon. It was a time when Piruz, in between trips to his newly purchased orchard on the shore of the Caspian Sea, would sometimes try to manipulate her by offering to take little Nader out. It was an obvious tactic to avoid arguing over disagreeable family matters, like budgeting and parenting. A bribe, a tactic, a trick—whatever it was, Yalda accepted it, despite her hesitation, with some suppressed anger. She'd already learned that something was better than nothing. Although she didn't trust Piruz to take care of her Little Bird, she'd let them go so that she could have a break and work on her own project for a few hours. She was so exhausted from shouldering all the responsibilities of her family that she sometimes felt like she hated both of them, Piruz and Nader, and along with them, all the people on the planet. When they came back home with ten stitches under little Nader's chin, she directed her hatred at herself for letting her Little Bird out of her sight. That evening, after Piruz explained what had happened, her hatred returned to its original target: a careless dad who had forgotten the baby while playing Frisbee.

Lying motionless on the beach, Yalda begins to feel the sun's golden needles pricking her. She grabs her purse and puts it to the side, takes off her sunglasses, and rolls over onto her stomach. Leaning her face against her palm, she picks up a handful of sand with her free hand and holds it tight to feel its warm solidity before loosening her grip to let it dribble through her fingers.

"Poor boy! He must have a father," said Sister Eti. They were in Essen, and it was the first time they had seen each other in fifteen years. Yalda restrained herself from saying, "How could I follow Piruz when he left his job and family to seclude himself in a tangerine orchard along the seashore?" Eti, kissing and caressing little Nader, who was exhibiting a new shyness towards strangers, repeated this remark over and over during the year they stayed in Essen.

And each time she heard Eti's prickly reminder, she would wonder what her older stepsister, who could have been her mother with their twenty-year age gap, really meant. Was she implying that Yalda should make up with Piruz, or find a substitute for him? Yalda had chosen to be a single mother, and she found her stepsister's comments annoying, if not offensive. To avoid a bitter argument, she refused to ask for clarification. Before arriving in Essen, Yalda had promised herself to be careful not to get trapped in any awkward conversations with Eti. She had even made a list of strictly forbidden topics: the murder of Dadash Yunes, the execution of her Nader, and the affiliations of Sister Eti's son, Kami, with SAVAK. She had considered other potential hosts and destinations in Europe, and Eti in Essen, she now admits, was eventually chosen by her head, not her heart. In the back of her mind, she had assumed that Sister Eti's husband had squandered away their inheritance from Agha Jun. Hadn't he tried to invest their money in growth stock, and failed? It had always bothered her that afterward Dadashi had been forced to quit school to make a living. Nevertheless, from her sister's perspective, family bonds came first and foremost. From Yalda's point of view, Sister Eti was still wealthy, and her apartment would therefore be the best place for her son. His welfare was her main priority. Yalda thought that Eti would feel the same way, and that their agreement in this respect would ease the long-term discomfort in their relationship. Yalda saw two more advantages to living with Eti: her stepsister was living alone after the death of her husband, and she was not in touch with her son Kami and his family, despite living in the same town. For this, Yalda, without remorse, was thankful to someone called "that termagant" by Sister Eti. "That termagant" was Sister Etil's daughter-in-law, who had effectively cut Eti out of Kami's life.

Her eyes closed, Yalda runs the sand through her fingers and tries to picture her stepsister's face. Nothing pops into her mind. She keeps trying, but she can't seem to imagine it. Not Sister Eti in her heyday, when Yalda saw her as an intrusive older stepsister, or in Essen, when Yalda saw her as a woman who had been destroyed and was living in exile. Nor was she able to call up an image of Sister Eti in her last days, when her only child, Kami, was too busy to visit her on her deathbed and Yalda was miles away in Saint-Étienne, rushing between *l'école* and the lingerie store and the den in her small flat.

Even though she can't picture Eti, Yalda can remember that she looked different in Essen. She was in her fifties, but she looked as if she had fast-forwarded to her seventies. She had craggy lines on her sagging skin, a paper-thin triple chin, flabby layers of fat around her bust, and a full head of thin silver hair. But the biggest change in Sister Eti was her new, lenient tone of voice; it had replaced the habitually stern tone that Yalda remembered from her childhood.

"Poor boy! He must have a father."

Yalda hears Eti's words in her head again, but now, to her surprise, she finds them wrapped in sympathy. Eti's comment had come at the end of a hard day with little Nader—he had had a tantrum after Eti had been unable to help him climb the slide in the nearby playground. The words, disappearing with a sudden warm breeze, leave Yalda pinned to the ground. Lying on the mat with the sound of the beach in her ears, she sees herself: plopped down on the mustard yellow couch in

Eti's living room, which looked as gloomy as the dull grey day slinking by outside the window. Hearing Eti's remark, she felt a brief panic. Her Little Bird, as still as a small statue, sitting in a W position on the floor, had his back to her and Eti and his face to the TV. Sister Eti, looking down at the incomplete crochet project on her lap, was perched on the antique love seat that had been overly decorated with small white crocheted doilies. She looked like a big-bellied Buddha, except that she was clearly unhappy. Eti's lips, pursed together, seem to be sealed for good after her remark. The image, unable to last, disappears from Yalda's mind. Bitterly, she remembers the fear she felt for the first time on that ash grey evening in Essen. It is a fear that has never left her: that growing up without a father would negatively impact her son.

Although she had resolved to ignore her remarks from day one, on that grey and gloomy day Eti's words succeeded in targeting her conscience and damaging her confidence as a capable single mother. The crack was tiny and the cut was minor, but both kept growing over the years. Now, she has to admit that they hurt a lot.

Crushed dream, crushed willpower. Yalda touches the grains of sand with her fingertips, feeling the sun on her back. She rolls over to open her eyes and face the great illuminator who's going to blind all her greedy admirers. To have her last words with the sun, Yalda sits up and puts on her sunglasses so she can maintain eye contact. The blue-green lake looks like a narrow strip on the bottom edge of the sun's skirt.

Recalling "Come Thou, Almighty King," she murmurs: *Come thou, Almighty Queen, light up the dark depths of this silenced sea!*

22.

CLEAN, QUIET, AND COOL. Yalda is pleasantly surprised that the washroom in the underground mall at Yonge and Bloor is up to her standards. "If nowhere else, in a washroom luxury can be justified," she says to herself, considering the shiny cleanliness and the velvet touch of the toilet paper.

Even though her position as an architect is uncertain, she still thinks she is the right person to claim that the public lavatory and the public library are the indexes of civilization. When she mentioned this idea to Michael, her boss, he had joked that it was a product of her third-world background rather than her vocational expertise. He can go to hell, Yalda thinks, and stay there until the further notice.

"Today is not your day, my dear boss!" Yalda says, closing the stall door. "And certainly, with your permission, I'm going to kick you out of my mind and focus on relaxing."

With her free hand, she hangs her purse on the hook, pulls at the roll of toilet paper, and disposes the first square into the trash bin. She folds a couple of squares and places them on the dispenser to hold the wet paper she is carrying in her other hand.

"This innovative cleaning method of a third world animal deserves a patent," she says to herself, hovering above the toilet and removing every bit of urine with wet toilet paper. "And it is the only good thing I've discovered from being born into a Muslim family."

Before leaving the washroom, her eyes catch her image in the mirror. She pauses to take a look at her watch. It's around the time that Dan should be in the bar.

"Not the time to think about him, though," she says under her breath.

Putting her purse on the glossy marble counter, she stands in front of a mirror that, regardless of the light, looks flattering enough to show her what she wants to see. She smiles, appreciating the fact that this mirror doesn't seem to want to reflect her imperfections, as mirrors so often do.

Nonetheless, I don't owe this good-looking face just to you, mirror, she thinks.

Yalda has been having a good day so far, beginning with the morning sunshine and its warm velvet touch.

She pulls her long-forgotten makeup bag out of her purse to see what sort of fast renovation she can do. No concealer, no foundation, no eye shadow or eyeliner. She starts with moisturizer, applies it in dots over her face in the style of crossing oneself, and blends it in with her fingertips.

After the sunshine, it was the half-open door of Nader's room, propitious after being kept closed for such a long time, that has made this a good day. This marked either a good omen or a sign of a promising change in his mood, and it also made her happy to see her son sleeping in the familiar fetal position. For a moment, she had a feeling that the present was the continuation of the past when she was full of hope for her Little Bird—as if there had never been a dark gap between now and then, him and her.

She notices that she still has some waterproof mascara left in the tube. Covering her lashes with two thin coats, she recalls her unexpected conversation with Dan. It doesn't make her blush, but it does remind her of a Leonard Cohen song. Applying a shade of blush to the apples of her cheeks—being careful not to make herself into a Russian *matryoshka*—she hums the refrain, "*dance me to the end of love.*"

Back above ground, the song is replaced by traffic noise. The parking lot, where she can jump into her car to head home, and the tapas bar, where she can join a man who's waiting for her, are both in the same direction. She puts off making up her mind. Instead, she replays her conversation with Dan this morning in the office kitchen.

"So you know the trick!" His voice sounded sweetly familiar. Before turning towards him, she paused to hide her excitement.

"Yes, I do." She avoided eye contact. "I had a guru once who taught me that, to have a hot cup of coffee, I had to fill my cup with boiling water first."

"I think I know your guru," Dan said with a smile more evident in his eyes than his lips.

"I didn't have just one guru," she said, gently shaking the cup full of boiling water to make it as hot as possible.

"I know the one who used to wait for his follower in the dim corner of a Spanish tapas bar," Dan said, filling his big mug with boiling water.

"Say hello to him, if you happen to see…"

"No, I won't." Dan interrupted her. When she turned towards him to make eye contact, he continued, with a bright smile on his face. "You can say hello to him yourself tonight before going home. His haunt is not far from here."

"We'll see," she said with an awkward smile.

Then, distracted by his decisiveness rather than his words, she grabbed her cup and turned to leave the kitchen. When she felt her hand burning, she heard Dan's soft, yet forceful, words, "He'll be waiting for you right at seven."

I bet Dan is still there, she thinks, looking down at her watch and following the movement of the second hand. Smiling back at the peach-faced waitress as she brings her a glass of wine, Yalda wonders if time is chasing after her or she is chasing after it. She takes off her watch and tosses it into her purse, resisting the temptation to run off to meet him before it's too late.

"*Pas de regrets!*" Yalda says under her breath before wetting her lips with red wine, which the waitress had chosen at her request.

She lets others choose for her whenever making decisions seems like a burden. But what if no one is available to carry the weight? So far, whenever she has been faced with two unpleasant options, she has always sought a third option. Fleeing the country with her son without giving Piruz notice is a clear example of this method. She used it to confront the biggest double bind in her life: staying in her devastating marriage for the sake of her Little Bird, or divorcing for her own sake and losing custody of her only child. The third option, that had once seemed promising, now looks useless. Nonetheless, the method of introducing a third option, which she first learned from Piruz, is still one she tends to apply. True to form, Yalda decided not to go to the parking lot or to the tapas bar. Instead, she kept going straight and eventually found the empty back patio of a cozy café—far from Dan and anyone other than herself.

"It's no wonder that muddy feelings lead you down a muddy road," she murmurs, feeling the mild sting of an ignored desire.

Even if it was the right time for her to be with a man, that man would not be Dan. She remembers that she had the same thought the first time they had gone on a date. In the first moments, her misbehaving brain compared him to Marc. Right in the middle of their conversation he'd asked, "Is this a date?" Returning his alluring smile with an ironic one, she'd replied, "*Ceci n'est pas une pipe.*" And when an awkward expression appeared on his face, she felt a sense of disappointment at their lack of compatibility. That night, in the loneliness of her bed, the angel of fairness pinched her and made her admit it was not fair to compare Dan with Marc. She shouldn't expect a marketing man to decode the language of art.

Yet their incompatibility was not all about their different backgrounds, or even their lack of common interests. The big obstacle to her desire for intimacy with him was not that he was a married man, but a scene that she had witnessed one rainy night and that had stuck in her head ever since.

On that rainy night, Yalda had been on her way to an end-of-project party for the firm. She and Dan had been on a successful date only the day before. Outside the restaurant, she had paused to watch Dan and his wife enter. They were chatting and giggling, taking shelter under his black umbrella. Not enough room for a *maîtresse*, she'd decided then.

Then she remembers how another scene ended her relationship with Marc, and guzzles her wine. It occurs to her that the impact of images on her mind was stronger than that of morals. She closes her eyes to revive the image, and it appears in her mind's eye like an old vintage photo: the veranda of Marc's ranch house where he and Yalda were relaxing after a charrette. As she bent to give him a kiss, she spotted his wife in her wheelchair coming around the corner.

"I'm not cold-hearted enough to compete with a woman confined to a wheelchair because of a stroke," Yalda says under her breath and opens her eyes to the dusk falling over the city.

23.

"NO. NOBODY IS OVER THERE," Yalda mutters out loud, swallowing this bitter pill at the end of her bad day. I'm not finished yet, she thinks, taking her eyes off the bar stools. Two of them are occupied by men: one has a long, braided ponytail, and the other has messy curly hair. By "nobody" she means the man with the shaved head, a familiar stranger—the shadow man—the man she was hoping to see. She has only seen the shadow man once before, a year ago. How is it possible that she now wishes to see him again?

Lingering on the threshold of the pub, she ponders what made her leave the tapas bar and end up here. Fear of running into Dan at the bar is a shallow excuse. Since their last short talk in the office kitchen, she hadn't seen him. An hour ago, in the tapas bar, she looked at her watch after her second drink and thought it was time for Dan to be in his living room, surrounded by his wife and his four daughters. Dan was a dutiful family man. For her, as a forsaken single woman, it was time to head to another tavern.

"On that summer day, the moment my feet took me somewhere other than the tapas bar, it was clear that Dan didn't stand a chance," she concludes.

She casts her eyes over to the seat where she'd seen, or maybe imagined, the shadow man last year. The corner leather sofa, her snug hideout, is now occupied by a couple half-hidden behind the pillar. The pillar reminds her that the jinn might be waiting in ambush, as she was last year.

"If she comes to visit me, we can celebrate the anniversary of the big bang," she sneers.

Her jinn, as it happens, doesn't bother to appear. Yalda turns to the counter. This evening will not be a copy of last year. No sign of the jinn, no punk waiter, and no man with a shaved head.

She wants to go out. The average-looking bartender, smiling at her and catching her eye, encourages her to change her mind and leads her to the counter. The wind is blowing outside, waiting to slap her in the face with a snappy, airy hand, but a dry martini will give her the fuel she needs to face the night.

I'm not going to get drunk on just one martini, she thinks, caressing the curve of the glass with her bloodless fingertips. Her eyes follow the bartender as he wends his way to the other end of the counter to check in on the two men. At the tapas bar, she ordered a beer after hours of wandering around town. This was her attempt to digest the devastating remorse she felt after her burst of anger. But she didn't feel able to enjoy her drink in solitude. She wasn't really a beer drinker, and she was plagued with thoughts of Dan.

Retreating into the corner a bit more, Yalda turns to the other side, slouches over the shiny wood, puts her elbows on the counter, and assumes a protective posture with her head leaning against her palm.

She has no one to go to for solace at the end of a terrible day. Without a doubt, she should keep herself sane and sober. On impulse, she takes the first sip of her drink and bites her wet lower lip hard enough to taste the saltiness of blood.

Earlier, in the morning, the day hadn't looked ominous. When she passed by the half-closed door of Nader's room, she let out a sigh of relief that at least the situation hadn't gotten worse. Never losing faith in her son, she was reluctant to recognize that this was the calm before a new storm. It was her last day off after a stressful charrette, and she was planning to prepare his favourite dish when she got home from her errands. Her first errand was to stop by the office to check in about a new project. The second one was to pick up Nandita and Rima at the corner of Yonge and Bloor and, together with them, visit Asuntha, who was in a mental health centre downtown.

"Then that damn thing turned my day upside down," she says, addressing her drink.

Yalda wonders what had triggered her unrestrained anger. After Negative Judy announced that Michael hadn't included Yalda in the new project, she had remained silent. Staring at Judy's mouth as she spoke, Yalda felt a kind of revulsion. However, outside the office, she filled her lungs with chilly air. She pushed aside the image of Judy's face, as well as her hostile feelings towards Michael and her recurring worries about her finances. She was determined to get back on track. Remembering Nader's open door, she felt hopeful that they might be able to take a little step forward to fix their damaged relationship.

"No, that asshole, Michael, could not beat me," she mutters, while taking a quick sip of her drink.

She admits to herself that, as difficult as it was for her, the episode in the office was not the cause of her sudden anger. At the corner of Yonge and Bloor, when she found Nandita alone, she hadn't been able to guess what had happened. Even as Nandita enumerated her worries about Rima, Yalda had refused to let them sour her day. She reminded herself that, unlike her Maman Ashi, she was not a woe-is-me type of woman. That Rima had gone back home was not bad news, per se. No! When Nandita told her about Rima's intention to go to the notorious Abu Ghraib dungeon, it didn't sound bad to her at all. For a mother looking for her son, a shot in the dark was better than nothing. In the mental health ward, she watched Nandita feed Asuntha her homemade date-and-fig *karanji*. Asuntha's wide-open eyes were unbearably cold; and Yalda felt her positivity falter and freeze in its tracks. The cold front coming from Asuntha's eyes, along with the clouds around Rima's trip, brought her down but didn't make her boil over.

Then Yalda remembers the final incident of the day. Recalling how her sudden fury made the fresh shrimp fly out of the plastic bag and spatter around the kitchen, Yalda raises the glass to her lips to swallow her shame. Entwined with alcohol, the shame running through her veins revives her rage against herself. "Fucking mom!" she says under her breath, repeating Nader's heinous words.

No, he didn't say mom, she thinks. She takes another gulp of her drink, steeling herself to repeat his words: "...fucking nightmare!" He grunted it with overt disgust. It was such a short response to her long, angry lecture. It was the final blow.

She stretches her hand towards the glass. It's empty. She opens her mouth to order another one, but quickly bites her lips hard enough to suppress the craving for more alcohol. She asks for the bill. Yes, it would be best to keep herself sane and sober. She has nobody by her side to save her from going back home. Her fight with Nader was devastating, but she knows that to go home to an empty house, a house without Nader, would be unbearable.

Feeling the slap of wind on her face, her heart aches for her son. The fact that he has left her home is nothing compared to the pain of losing him in such a ridiculous way. As if she has been stabbed in the back, Yalda drags her feet on the sidewalk. She keeps thinking about her dashed hopes, her wrecked expectations. "Is it too much to ask to not see my son with a weapon?" She repeats the same question over and over.

That afternoon, she opened the door and saw him trying on a bulletproof vest and duty belt in front of the mirror.

All she said at first was, "what are you doing to yourself?" He didn't say anything in reply, just gave her a cold look. She repeated the question, this time more loudly and with undisguised rage. It was his coldness that caused her anger and despair to boil over.

Her anguish, which had caused the shrimp to fly around the kitchen and the hallway, is now beating in her head. She replays what she had said to him:

"You don't understand what I mean. I gave birth to a human being. I can't stand seeing my son with a weapon that is nothing but a tool for killing. It's not just a thing hanging from your belt. It's something that makes you a target to be shot at, or that makes you shoot at a target. It's not about good guy, bad guy; it's about this damn thing....

"Think of me as an asshole, a fanatic woman from a backward country, but don't expect me to let my son go around carrying a gun, even in the name of defence or in the name of good."

As her thoughts speed by, out of her control, she looks around helplessly. In the distance, she spots a cop patrolling the street. Pausing to change direction, it occurs to her that, again, she has no choice but to flee. An approaching cab appearing before her looks like a miraculous means of escape.

"Nirvana." This is what slips out of her mouth as the driver looks at her expectantly. "Please hurry!"

The driver doesn't take his foot off the brake or his eyes off her.

"It's somewhere around Montreal," Yalda fabricates. She notices that he doesn't look Indian.

"Bus terminal or train station?" asks the driver.

"Oh, no!" Yalda pauses. "I'm going to drive there. But first I have to go home."

24.

"WHY DID I END UP HERE?" Although the question is a sign that Yalda is beginning to regain her senses, she is unable to find an answer. Though recently she's often asked herself, "*how did I end up here?*" now she notices that "how" is replaced with "why." Lying under a dull red blanket, she half-opens her eyes to see a pale spot in front of her eyes. She's tempted to think of it as the light at the end of the tunnel, but her brain encourages her to avoid illusions. On the other hand, it also refuses to answer her questions—routine ones like "what day is it today?" and "what am I supposed to do today?" as well as biting ones like "why did I end up here?"

Huddled under the shadow man's blanket, Yalda awkwardly finds herself in the fetal position—reminiscent of her lost birdie. She stretches her back and straightens her legs to relieve the pain in her stiff body. Rolling onto her stomach, she pulls the pillow out from between her knees to put it underneath her. The hard floor tells her that she must have fallen asleep at the shadow man's table once again. By now she's named it her "altar," the place where she will perform her rites. The small square table looks just like a worn-out Japanese tea table. Staring at it, she sits up, her body still wrapped and her head peeking out from under the blanket. She looks towards the half-open curtain, beyond which she can see the shadow man's bed. Throwing the pillow towards the empty bed, she recalls her own pillow, once high in demand and now forsaken in an abandoned apartment. She wonders if Nader misses the pillow, too.

Trying to ignore the sudden rush of self-pity, she turns her eyes away from the pillow and towards the altar. A couple of days after the shadow man left her alone in his studio, she made up her mind to listen to his advice about not ending up in a mental institution. It was the day she went to the clinic to have her sutures removed. On her way back to the shadow man's cave, she'd resolved to get better. She started with the thing that came easiest to her: cleaning therapy. The Lilliputian atelier of a traveller shadow man didn't offer much of a chance to scrub or mop or dust, but she did what she could. Gradually, the cluttered space became peaceful, and the table that had been hidden under a pile of paper became the altar for the method of meditation that she invented herself.

"Sorry, dear Buddha, for distorting your teaching," she says under her breath. "After all, as an Iranian, I can't help tampering."

Placing her hand on the edge of the table—she needs to be in contact with wood, the agent of Mother Nature—she recalls her first and last trip to the Holy Site, *Haram,* in Qom. She had accompanied the two most important women in her life at the time: Maman Ashi and Sister Eti. As she meditates, images and smells come back to her: dazzling metals and mirrors, Maman Ashi's broken face in its cancer shock phase, the weird mix of body odour and rosewater, Sister Eti's made-up face among countless crude faces of helpless pilgrims, the *zarih,* or outer enclosure of the holy shrine, which was solid and impassable under the touch of fingers and lips and foreheads. She wondered what made her a heretic—that the *zarih* looked like a cage, or that the unseemly pile of coins and bills on top of the hidden tomb of a saint was in stark contrast to the dire poverty of large numbers of pilgrims.

When Sister Eti commanded her, with a look, to kiss a hard-to-find knob of the *zarih*, Yalda decided she would not worship a money-taking saint, nor would she touch the glittering metal that reflected the distorted faces of its adorers.

Being careful not to irritate her new scar, she rests her forehead on her altar to pray for protection from the demon of madness. Yet the mind, a disbelieving monkey, doesn't relax in any cage. She murmurs and mutters *nirvana*, her new mantra, and suddenly feels as stupid as those pilgrims in the *Haram* with their moving lips, shaking heads, and blank gazes.

The more you repeat a word, the more it sounds hollow, she thinks. And once again, she feels like her nirvana is getting thinner and paler. Soon there will be nothing left but delirium.

"A pathetic cheater like me doesn't deserve nirvana," she says under her breath.

It was nirvana itself, though, that slipped out of her mouth when the cab driver in Toronto asked her where to go.

Hell was back at home, and heaven was out of the question, so where else could she go but nirvana? It's the only place that would be a haven for a helpless cynic, she thinks.

In the cab, it suddenly occurred to her that Montreal was calling her. When the car stopped in front of the building, she'd already made up her mind to get into her own car and head to nirvana. She somehow knew that the road would pass through Montreal.

In the elevator, she noticed the up arrow was lit and felt a beam of hope dart into her gloomy mind. Although she knew it wasn't likely that he had returned home, her desire for nirvana faded.

Lifting her head from the altar, Yalda looks around to spot her most recent mantra, which she had written down. The papers, organized in bunches, are sitting next to each other in a semi-circle around her altar. She counts them. This is her way of keeping track of time, of how many days have passed since she dedicated herself to the question, "How did I end up here?" She sought an answer to the question by applying her own version of *vipassana*: an eclectic technique of Iranian *zij-neshini* (creeping in a corner), *à la mode de chez une femme laique,* Indian meditation methods, and the voodoo practised by West Indians. Her rites are made up of all the techniques and tricks known to her. This all takes place in the solitary confinement offered to her by the shadow man, a stranger who'd asked for another tale in lieu of rent.

"Instead of weaving a tale for you, man, I've *woodled* (a combination of weaving and doodling) my fifty years of life in three weeks," Yalda murmurs, picking up and browsing through a bunch of papers, each revolving around a flashback.

Feeling the urge to reach thirty pieces in the thirty-day timeslot offered to her by the shadow man, she wonders if this makes her superstitious.

"Not done yet," she says to herself, surveying the papers in front of her.

Her *woodles,* which are the core of her *zij-neshini,* are supposed to clear up the muddle that she's found herself in. Now it occurs to her, though, that these scrambled words and notes and lines and figures are as odd as the papers of talisman writers. She remembers the day Dadash Yunes found out Maman Ashi had hidden some papers by a talisman writer under the rug of his room. It had so angered him that it had led to his final quarrel with Maman Ashi. She closes her eyes for a moment. The face of Dadash Yunes, purple with rage, appears next to Maman Ashi's chalky white one.

When the images fade and the colours dissolve into dark, she recalls her silence when Dadash Yunes asked her what she thought of Maman Ashi's stupid, superstitious plot to ruin his prospective marriage with Turan, their neighbour's daughter. She shuffles and piles the papers in the centre of the altar. The note about enmity between Dadash Yunes and Maman Ashi catches her eye. Fixing her eyes on it, she recollects another conversation she once had with Dadash Yunes:

"Dadashi, why didn't you come to my place with Ensi? I was looking forward to meeting my only sister-in-law."

"Really? I thought you had no interest in getting to know my wife."

"Why would you think that?"

"Sis, neither you nor your Sister Eti came to my wedding."

"It was just a month after Maman Ashi's death."

"How did I forget that?" He was sarcastic.

"Well, Maman Ashi is not alive anymore, so you cannot hurt her with your words."

"But she still hurts me, even after her death."

"How?"

"How? Wasn't it because of things she'd said that you didn't come to my wedding?"

"I wasn't in the mood to go to a party. That's all."

"Really?"

"Well, she didn't want you to get married, to Turan or to anybody else."

"You're not a good liar, Sis. Is that all?"

"Yes. I don't know what things you heard about her. She was just cranky as hell in her final months with colon cancer, knowing that all she was leaving behind was a teenaged daughter."

"You're good at making excuses. Is that all?"

"Well, she didn't like her stepson, and you don't like your dead stepmother."

"I'm talking about something else."

"Okay, fine. You want to hear it from me? She looked down on your wife's family. She used to say that it was a shame you were going to marry a girl whose father had been the doorman at your father's factory."

"Aha! My high-born stepmother didn't see that after she squandered my father's wealth, the doorman became a prosperous landlord!"

"It's too bad!"

"What's too bad? That our father's doorman is now loaded and we're penniless?"

"That you can't forgive your pitiful stepmother."

Yalda scribbles out the note so that she can no longer read what she had written about Dadash Yunes and Maman Ashi. The resentment between them reminds her of her own relationship with her son. She stabs her pencil into the paper and bites her lips.

"*Addle ... waddle ... doodle doo woodle voodoo....*" The broken words pouring out of her bitten lips don't make much sense. Once again, like what she sees in her dreams, the path begins with her murdered brother and ends with her lost son. It seems to her that her mind has been manipulated by her brother. She remembers that Dadash Yunes used to draw a long line with a piece of charcoal on the white plaster walls of narrow alleys in her childhood neighbourhood. At the end of the line, he would draw a thumbs-up sign. He thought it was fun to make a fool of those kids who followed the line on the walls. This time, the line leads her to her teenaged son, obsessed with video games, hunched over his computer in their small studio in the McGill Ghetto. He feels so close yet so agonizingly far. This image is the only one that flashes into her mind from that Montréal period, when she spent her days sorting out bras and panties in a lingerie stockroom and her evenings drafting labouriously for half the going rate. The only other thing she recalls is the constant physical fatigue. It was relieved only by the pride of being a single mother who was capable of providing her child not only with food and a home, but also with a good education at an English school with a hefty tuition fee.

"I was living my life like a blindfolded animal," she says to herself. Her chest tightens. "Now I'll never see my son again, never ever...."

A surge of disappointment courses through her veins and makes her reach for her cellphone, in her purse under the altar. When her hand touches cold metal, she feels a shiver running down her spine. She pulls the hammer out of the purse and stares at it. She got it from a dollar store on her last day wandering around the city. Immediately afterwards, she suddenly felt the urge to call her son from a pay phone. She forgot all about the hammer, and it remained buried in her purse.

"Only the devil knows why I got a hammer," she whispers. "Not just because it reminded me of that damn hammer and my poor brother."

Putting the made-in-China hammer over the pile of papers, she digs out her phone. A new obsessive thought enters her mind. Gingerly, she picks up her tiny black phone and stares at it. After Nader had slammed the door behind him, it became a source of hope and horror: he will call, he will not call. All of a sudden, she feels her blood running hot and fast in her veins.

I should have ignored the damn thing. Of all my resolutions after coming back from the clinic, to ignore my phone was supposed to be number one. Maintaining my solitude, following a sort of yogic diet, doing a mantra... What the hell is the point of all these if I'm still holding onto my phone? I'm such an imbecile. I've been hoping to hear it ring, linking me to him—a child who was already detached from me the moment the umbilical cord was cut. All these days and nights I've spent trying to repair the burned bridges with him, I've been dying to hear it ring. I've left messages every day for a month. Even though he hasn't returned any of them, I've still been holding out hope that he would reach out. Bah ... motherly stupidity or love or whatever! In the elevator, I took the lit arrow as a sign to justify my desperate longing for his return. I wanted to make up, to keep the door open ... but for what?

Did I want to have something to cling to? Or did I want to keep taking care of him and protecting him from evil? Oh, yeah! No longer a little bird, but a man rushing towards his prime. A man I need to look up to while my life is going downhill. The man I wanted to replace all the lost men of my life—everyone and everything I lost in the ashes of the past. That is not the whole story, though. What made me put off my trip to nirvana after finding his room empty was deeper than a sentimental mother's love. I wanted to keep the door open not only for me, but mostly for him. I left him a brief message with the most elaborate care, with no pathetic tone, no preaching, no trace of reproach: "I'm leaving for Montreal so that you can come back home. Please take care of the house and yourself!"

My words fell on deaf ears. As if he could not read my mind! Well, true, I did not want to see my Little Bird, my young man, stepping towards violence. Ah, all my running away! Wasn't it all to keep him safe from fights and fires? I was driven not to give up? Not only during my stay at the B&B on Saint-André, when I was stupid enough to send a plea to his voicemail, but also after that horrible day that brought me here, with a scar on my head. What an obnoxious person I am! An obsessed mom running after her baby to keep his ass clean!

Well, eventually I succeeded in reaching him from a pay phone. I kept begging and pleading for his mercy, if not his love, for him to come back home, if not back to me. Did I tell him the last thing I'd done before leaving was to put the pillow on his bed? Pooh, poor idiot, you used all your tricks; you made your mind go numb, and you were drowned. Yeah, I was drowning deeper and deeper, while all he said was, "It's over."

Yeah, yeah, yeah, when it's gone, it's gone. Somebody farted in the sky, and here, on the earth, I drowned in the depths of shit. Hours later, I found myself drunk in a tavern and heard the familiar voice from the person I was looking for in the Toronto pub. I hit my temple, I shaved my hair, I confined myself in a stranger's cell, but I didn't hear the damn phone ring! I should have thrown it away. I should have crushed it! It's ruined my own vipassana. *I have failed to see myself as I am, let alone to see him as he is....*

Yalda feels as if lead, rather than blood, is being forced through her veins. She calls forth all her stamina, shoves the blanket away, and gets up. With the phone in her hand, she casts her eyes at the hammer that is now a paperweight holding down the papers on the table.

I didn't get this hammer to smash my cell phone, she thinks.

She throws the phone to the ground and tries to crush it under her foot. Hurting her heel, she gives up and distracts herself by turning towards the small window. The grey daylight filters in through glass covered with a grimy canvas curtain. Behind the curtain, there is a bowl of almonds on the windowsill—out of sight, out of mind. Dragging her feeble feet towards it, she wonders if there are any left. She lets her hand creep up and reach into the bowl without pulling the curtain aside, as if this will mean that she is obeying the rules of *vipassana*. She finds the bowl empty and, for some reason, gets butterflies in her stomach.

"Empty bowl, empty belly," she mutters. She hits her belly with clenched fists, taking out her anger and anxiety on the womb that had once nourished her Little Bird.

25.

"WHAT A DAY!" SHE EXCLAIMS OUT LOUD. The expression, repeating itself, this time at the end of the day, reminds her of this morning when she ended her three-week *zij-neshini* and went out. The fresh taste of the outdoors after hibernation! There was a sort of soothing feeling of being part of the crowd again, just at the moment when she was becoming most aware of her loneliness.

It feels good when nobody around you recognizes you as an alien, she thinks.

Yet she was not different from the people who surrounded her. On the street, everybody, in a car or on foot, had something to do: going to work, running a business, shopping for Christmas, or doing an errand. She also had a series of tasks to complete, including throwing her cellphone into the trash and fueling her empty stomach with fruit juice and a fresh Montreal bagel. She needed to find an ATM to check her meagre savings account and take her car out of the public parking lot. She planned to get gas and ride her silver horse around the city in the hope of visiting their old haunts. It seemed to her that the places, once too close to be seen, are now too far to be touched. These included the studio, the private English school, the lingerie store, the office of this or that architecture firm, and a café downtown where Nader told her on their first day in the city that he would not go to a French school. There was also the café in Old Montreal where she told him they were

going to have to move again, this time to Springfield, because she'd gotten a job offer from a fairly well-known architect.
 So she had things to do, just like everyone else. And she was one of many on the street, in the city, on the earth that was turning nonstop, always moving from dark to light and from day to night.
 It was a dull day with a brutal cold in the air, blemished white snow banks here and there, and withered twigs on trees against a grey horizon. But she was glad to note that the sky was not falling and it was not pouring.

And now? Ah! With her back against a wall, and her arms around her knees, she looks over the special small *sofreh*. She feels pretty good. The *sofreh*, a white cotton scarf that she found in the glove compartment, is now spread on the floor, between the wall and the altar. The poor altar is still enduring the burden of her incomplete woodles, which are, in turn, being weighed down by the yet-to-be-used club hammer. In order to keep the altar pristine, she spread her meal out on the *sofreh*: a cold dish of mortadella and mustard and Jewish pickles, with a baguette and booze. The meal is modest, yet enough to soothe a lonely night; she hardly expects any company, even her own jinn, who hasn't visited her at all since Yalda spotted her in the back seat of the car on the trip to Montreal.
 "Drinking *à la mode de chez* Agha Jun," she says to herself with a chuckle.
 She wonders why, at the end of her time in the city, instead of creeping into a smoky, noisy tavern, she ended up at a familiar deli to buy supplies for a solitary feast. Entering the store, she recalled the evening she'd bought mortadella there with all the money in her purse to surprise Nader with a different type of dinner. When he didn't show any interest, she asked him what he would have preferred.
 "Hm! The self-sacrificing mom insisted on going back to

the store to get what her Little Bird wanted," she says with a voice dripping with sarcasm.

His unexpected demand was too hard, though. It made her willingness to please him evaporate in a flash. Nader, seeming eager to ignite an old beef, had started teasing her about her refusal to eat horsemeat salami. In the store, trying not to look at the salami rolls, she regretted being resentful of a teenage boy who didn't have anybody to challenge other than a frazzled single mom. She didn't regret buying salami, even for her Little Bird. He already knew that she loved horses. When it comes to love, fairness flies out of the window. Too bad that her argument against eating *saucisson de cheval* failed to convince either her son or the animals, whose meat in the glass display was trying to catch her attention.

Right now, a few slices of mortadella on a neat white *sofreh* trigger memories of Agha Jun. Among all those she had lost, nobody could have been further from her mind than Agha Jun. Recalling her father's solemn eating and drinking ritual, she swallows her first bite. She digs a portable CD player out of her purse along with a few CDs she had brought from the car—she had decided to add music to her last evenings in the cell. She plugs in the CD player and flips through the CDs. Among them, *The Fountain* soundtrack is not a random choice. Not because it is one of her favourite CDs, but because over the last year it was the only music that could soothe her turbulent soul.

"If the CD hadn't kept me company, my road trip to Montreal might have ended in a handy nirvana," she says aloud. "It prevented me from having a fatal car accident."

The moment requires another choice, though—*The Fountain* demands her full attention, but she finds herself distracted by thoughts of Agha Jun. She picks up an old CD by Banan, a prominent traditional music singer of Agha Jun's generation whose songs were an indispensable part of his drinking ritual. With Banan's sonorous voice spreading around and filling the silence at a low volume, Yalda closes her eyes. She pictures the gramophone on the mahogany table in the *talar*, the big guest room. Agha Jun didn't sit in the guest room; it mostly remained closed to the members of the household so that it would be neat and clean for high-ranking visitors. He used to sit in the next room, the *panj-dari*, a room with five doors that opened onto the courtyard. He would keep the door to the *talar* open when he wanted to listen to a record. The *panj-dari*, a favourite room in the house, was a place where East met West. The traditional doors with their stained-glass windows looked out on the *howz*, which was nestled in the heart of flower beds in the courtyard. On the other side of the room was their old-fashioned radio, the venerable ambassador of the modern world, magnificently throned on the plaster mantelpiece. There was also a dining table with a flannel-backed plastic tablecloth that was used by the family members; they weren't supposed to use the huge walnut dining table in the *talar*, which was just for guests. Although Agha Jun yielded to pro-Western influence by buying a dining table for the family, he still preferred to sit in front of a *sofreh* on the floor. Thanks to his interest in trendy furniture, as well as the influence of Mati, who advocated for a Western lifestyle, a compromise was eventually found: Agha Jun was allowed to eat a late lunch and dinner on his single *sofreh* spread on the floor for every meal except the formal family weekend lunch on Fridays.

"*À votre santé, cher monsieur!*" she murmurs, remembering the recurring disagreement among her siblings about what to call Agha Jun in public.

In private, Big Brain and Big Heart gave him different names, depending on the situation; "Big Fuel Provider" was the most common. Little Sis, though, used to following her leaders, mostly referred to her father as "he" or "him." When it came to what to call him in public, Mati argued that Agha Jun, who was called Gholam Khan by many, had a strange name. It was she, the most learned sibling, who first noticed that her stepfather's first name, Gholam (meaning "slave"), sounded ridiculous with a title like Khan, which meant "sir." Both Big Brother and Little Sis agreed. Mati, reluctant to call her step-father Agha Jun, also argued that the name's French equivalent, *cher monsieur*, sounded ridiculous too. When she proposed "Papa" as an alternative, Dadash Yunes, bursting into laughter, insisted that such a simple title would fly in the face of Agha Jun's authority. The final resolution, *Monsieur le Papa*, which met with the approval of the gang at once, was used for the first and last time that same evening when Agha Jun came home from work.

"Do you remember, Agha Jun, how you responded to it?" Yalda asks, taking another gulp of her drink. "You raised your ivory-handled cane, thrust it towards Dadash Yunes, and muttered, 'Never speak French in front of me again, son!'"

The cane didn't dance in the air to show his anger, as it did when Maman Ashi drove him nuts bragging about her noble roots and relatives. It was not beaten on the ground either, as it was when the foreman in the factory or one of the workers angered him. The cane, the wooden tongue of Agha Jun, as Big Brain used to say, was just used to punctuate an ordinary fatherly warning. The good thing about it, as Big Heart used to say, was that it was not used to hurt its owner's son.

"You were not a bad father, I have to admit, Agha Jun, but..." Yalda pauses to fill the glass for him, "...even for your son, or maybe particularly for him, you were a strange father."

And for little Yalda? To find the answer to such a question, she needs more alcohol. Her blood running more quickly, she recalls standing next to the girl next door, Turan, in the pale light of dawn, watching with wide eyes as pallbearers carried a dead body covered by a piece of *termeh* through the alley. She recognized the pattern on the Persian hand-woven cloth and knew that it was Agha Jun. The night before, Maman Ashi had closed the door of the *panj-dari*, where Agha Jun was sick in his temporary bed, and asked Dadash Yunes to take her to Sister Eti's house. Yalda refused to go, bursting into tears.

Dadashi convinced her to stay over at their nice neighbour's house with Turan.

"You've always been a stranger to me, Agha Jun." She lifts her glass. "Just like the dead body moving up and down on the pallbearers' shoulders. You filled the traditional role of the head of family: you kept your distance from us to appear authoritarian, and we kept our distance from you to avoid trouble, she thinks.

"Sorry, Agha Jun, I would never have imagined that years later I would have you as my drinking buddy," she says with a sheepish grin on her face, filling his glass. "You were never unkind to your kids." She pauses to take a long sip from his glass. Feeling warm under her skin, Yalda picks up a pickle before resuming the conversation with drunken frankness.

"Well, I'm telling you, Agha Jun. You were a pretty good father to me, but I have to tell you the truth. You had a bald head and a wrinkled face. I felt so unhappy I could not see you as a warm and loving daddy. Yeah, to be honest, when Mati showed me a photo of her young and handsome father with a Clark Gable haircut, I felt a sort of dislike for you, Agha Jun." This is an awkward confession, she thinks.

Unable to take a deep breath in the stuffy cell, Yalda rests her forehead on the edge of the altar. She closes her eyes and concentrates on the warm voice of Banan as it fills the room with charm. Once again, the image of Agha Jun appears, shaking his ivory-handled cane in the air and holding the club hammer in the other hand. Feeling a chill run down her spine, she opens her eyes and takes her head off the altar, trying to ignore what's on it.

"I'm drunk," she says under her breath, turning off the CD and silencing the love song.

"Nobody's in a romantic mood, Agha Jun. Am I right?" she asks, sniggering.

With a burning sensation in her stomach, she gobbles up another bite of her homemade sandwich, and craves some *mast-o-khiyar,* a Persian side dish that was an indispensable part of Agha Jun's *sofreh.*

"You liked the way Mati used to make it—yoghurt and cucumber with *kakuti,* the aromatic dried herb," she says, recalling how everything changed after the death of the Big Heart of the house.

"No, you never made a fuss over trivial things. You didn't mind when, after Mati's death, Maman Ashi didn't care about what you liked to eat," Yalda says, picking up breadcrumbs with the wet tip of her index finger the way her father had. "But it made you sulk. Well, after her death, all of us—not just you—in our own way began to feel sort of awkward in our skin. You were sullen; Dadashi and I were sad. And Maman Ashi? Well, she seemed quite savage after the loss of her tough cookie, her lovely moderator. It felt like, without Mati, we could no longer keep our balance on a tightrope and were about to bump into each other and collapse."

Taking the last sip of her drink, she falls silent, focusing on the agony she felt in a house where everybody needed Mati desperately, but nobody uttered her name.

"Nonetheless, Agha Jun, you didn't complain at all when Maman Ashi made your *mast-o-khiyar* not only without *kakuti,* but also without enough salt and pepper. You didn't say anything—maybe simply because you didn't want to ruin the pleasure of your solitary drinking."

Examining how much is left in the bottle, she recalls that it was during Mati's final months in bed that he switched from social drinking at Yezegel, the Jew's pub, to drinking alone at home. The children, knowing their parents' rule about drinking outside the home, were surprised. But they never investigated the mystery—the Big Heart of the house was feeble and the Big Brain of the house was confused. The youngest of the gang, though, unable to see the angel of death looming over Mati, could still hear the quarrelling between her parents behind the closed door.

"It was not easy for me to decode what was going on between you and Maman Ashi, you know, Agha Jun," she murmurs. "That she suspected you were going to the pub because of a cabaret dancer made you mad, I know. I still remember you yelling. You said that to see a dancer, one would go to the cabaret, not the pub." She laughs.

Eventually Maman Ashi stopped arguing with her husband and looked for a solution from her trusted advisors; among them, Sister Eti and her Turkish coffee fortune teller. What they decided remained a secret.

"And one evening you came home and began drinking alone, putting an end to your visits to Yezegel's," she says, still addressing Agha Jun and shaking her head. "Nobody, not even Big Brain, could guess why." She pauses to take a deep breath. "But little Yalda, Agha Jun—'the little bell for your coffin,' as Sister Eti used to say—happened to hear the story." She interrupts herself to take in more air. "Yes, Agha Jun, I heard Sister Eti saying that Maman Ashi bribed Yezegel to pee in your drink." She pauses again to swallow her saliva. "No, I didn't tell anybody, not even Dadashi. But years later, Agha Jun, when I asked Dadash Yunes why he didn't drink, he told me, 'Who knows? Any drink might be mixed with Yezegel's pee.'"

A sudden urge to puke makes Yalda get up and run to the bathroom. She kneels down and rests her hands on the edge of the toilet seat. She empties the contents of her stomach into the toilet. Feeling relieved, she gets up, splashes cold water on her face, and then wipes it brusquely with a towel. When she turns her head back to resume her conversation with Agha Jun, he is gone.

26.

OH, MY WHOLE BODY, FROM TOES TO NOSE, *feels stiff as wood. I sense, though, that there are layers of sleep clouds wrapping around my head. What a sweet inebriation they're bringing! I know my body is lying in a stranger's bed in Montreal. It's lying flat on its back like a dead body shrouded in a white sheet. I'm entranced, though, by the starlings' manoeuvres. It feels like they're in Rome. No, I'm not seeing myself sitting in a street café sipping espresso or watching people getting on and off the trams, or staring at the sacred ruins of Largo di Torre Argentina. I'm just gazing, as if through an imaginary kaleidoscope, at a flock of dark dots. Ah! They're turning and wheeling through the sunset-coloured firmament; they're forming ever-changing, mesmerizing shapes. They're....*

BUT THIS IS A DREAM!

And as soon as the thought occurs to her, darkness falls upon the earth and swallows the little dream. She sinks deeply into a calm ocean of nothingness, where she feels no weight and knows no time. When she resurfaces, she finds herself sitting in the same café in Centro Storico and sipping an aromatic Italian espresso. This time, as an indifferent observer, she is not doing anything other than enjoying her beverage while a series of images passes before her eyes.

Teatro di Pompeo. Yalda and little Nader are sitting in the audience. When the curtain goes up, the scene begins. Somebody grabs Yalda's shoulder. She hears an angry voice: "*Ista quidem vis est!*" She turns her face towards little Nader, saying, "but this is violence." She notices her son is missing. Frightened, she looks around and fixes her eyes on the stage. Not a *dictator perpetuo*, but a poor betrayed creature, tripping over the steps, utters her last words: "*Et tu, mon oisillon?*"

Via di Torre Argentina. Yalda waits in a queue for the tram. The cool breeze of a cloudy October day tousles the hair of two teenage girls who are chatting and chuckling. The on-duty street beggar at the tram stop, a one-legged boy on crutches, is staring at them with a wide smile on his narrow face. Yalda can't help looking at the empty trouser leg folded up and safety-pinned in the middle. That he is the same age as little Nader disturbs her.

Largo di Torre Argentina. Watching homeless cats meander in the ruins of that self-assured General Julius Caesar, Yalda remembers the Tehran of her childhood and its stray cats. In the basement or closet, under the staircase or on the roof, there was always a nervous mother cat ready to grab her baby by the scruff of the neck to carry it to safety.

"So, what does a dad cat do, Dadashi?"
"I'll tell you, Sis. He plants a seed and passes by."
"Shut up, Yunes!"
"Well, our little sis should learn about idle animals, Mati."
"You should stop harassing cats!"
"They eat my goldfish and my sparrows."
"Look at the mother cat on the wall! Don't you see how skinny she is from feeding?"
"Oh, poor mom!"
"She has to wander and wander and wander around looking for food and a home for her kitten. Don't you see her, Yunes?"

"I see her, Mati, but what does the kitten's dad do?"

Farmanieh, Tehran. Distracted from his book, Piruz rolls his eyes at little Nader. He is toddling and babbling non-stop, watching the trembling shadows of the cherry tree leaves on the wall. With one eye on her son and one on her studies, Yalda shrugs when Piruz asks her to stop Nader's prattling.

Dadash Yunes and his wife, Ensi, arrive with a bouquet of scarlet red and white gladiolus in hand. "This woman has no taste," Yalda mutters to herself as she looks for a vase in the kitchen cabinet. Like Piruz, who believes it is the flower of philistines, she dislikes the gladiolus. As much as she grumbles about her sister-in-law, she doesn't like anybody, particularly Piruz, putting down her brother and his family.

"Where are the kids?"

"They loved seeing your baby," Ensi replies.

"Goodness, even her voice hurts me," Yalda says under her breath.

Ensi has a nice face and blue eyes, but this isn't enough to win Yalda over. There is something about the look in her eyes and the ring of her voice that disturbs Yalda. She scolds herself for being so unfair to Ensi. She blames Maman Ashi for betraying her brother; she should not have conspired to make Turan turn her back on him! Turan was the right match, and Ensi is definitely the wrong one.

"Yunes didn't let them come with us," Ensi grumbles.

Dadash Yunes is considerate of Piruz, who doesn't like guests with children.

"Unexpected guests are intruders, and the immature ones are the worst," Dadash Yunes says to Piruz, laughing. "Isn't that right, Mr. Piruz?"

Ensi pulls her silky scarf over her forehead and protests. "Turaj and my Turan are not kids anymore, and Iran is not a naughty girl at all."

Ensi calls her daughter "my Turan" to distinguish her from

the other Turan. Yalda once told her brother that naming his daughter after his first love stung his wife. At this, Yunes shrugged. "I always planned to name my first daughter after my mother, Iran, the princess of Persia, and my second daughter after Turan, the princess of Iran's historical enemy, the Turks," he said. "As an overly considerate Iranian, I changed my mind and gave priority to my enemy to please my wife. After all, Ensi's grandmothers had some affairs with warriors of invading Turkish tribes."

Yalda finds a cheap crystal-like vase in the kitchen. In the other room, Yunes is saying to Ensi, "Stop yammering, lady princess, and let me play with this young man!"

"He never plays with his own kids," Ensi complains.

He can't help provoking her, and she can't help feeling jealous, Yalda thinks as she fills the vase with water.

"Where are you, Yalda? Come and see your birdie flying up in the air."

"Don't throw him in the air, Dadash Yunes!" Yalda runs toward the living room and stumbles over the step. Staring at the broken vase and scattered stems of gladiolus on the floor, Yalda hears Ensi screaming. All three men—Yunes, Piruz, and Nader—are laughing.

Niavaran Park, Tehran. Little Nader is toddling around on the soft sand of the playground. Yalda is happy, chatting with her brother, far away from the heavy presence of Piruz and letting her toddler practise this new skill. Dadash Yunes, scratching his chin, doesn't look as cheery as he usually does during his rare visits.

"Why is Ensi not happy with you, Dadash Yunes?"

"Hm! If the queen of complaints had half a brain in her head, she wouldn't bug you again."

"Your wife doesn't bug me."

"Don't forget she is the daughter of Haji—the man I hate the most."

"So what? When you proposed to her, didn't you know her father?"

"Then, he was the former doorman of my dad's factory with a sixteen-year-old daughter. For him, having a son-in-law with a government job was much better than being obligated to pay for the food and schooling of a teenage girl. Now, Haji is a stingy old miser kissing the *mullahs*' asses to guarantee his properties in this world and his seat in paradise."

"It doesn't matter that she is the daughter of a man you hate. She is your wife and the mother of your kids."

"She was born and raised in a family where tale-bearing and dissimulation, *taqiya,* are the rule. The devil knows how many times I have asked her not to piss in the ear of my sister when she visits once or twice a year."

"But she may have something to say."

"She has parents, plus a platoon of siblings, plus a brigade of relatives. I have only one dear little sister in the world who has a very noble and high-born husband."

"Stop being facetious, Dadash Yunes! You're annoying everybody with your poisonous language—not just the people you hate, but also the people you like."

"Am I annoying you, Little Sis?"

"It's not about me. In fact, it's about everybody. Please don't be so cynical. I understand that you feel disappointed in everybody and everything, but you can't change anybody or anything."

"That's why I'm calling a spade a spade."

"But don't you see that you're harming yourself first? Don't you see how you've damaged your skin with your damned nervous scratching?"

"Ha ha! What you see on my face is not skin. It's the hide of a rhino, which is what you need when the shit comes up to your neck. We're flouncing about in the crap of lousy *mullahs* who have ruined our country and our lives! Did you forget they killed your Nader for nothing? They're riding our backs thanks to superstition and ignorance and the greed of assholes like Haji."

"I'm talking about you, your wife, and your kids—not Haji or any other asshole."

"When she speaks, I hear Haji's voice. I hear him when she nags me about leaving my job in the air force after the *Anghollab* (literally, a sling that throws shit)—rather than *Enghelab*, the revolution—of *mullahs*."

"Well, I'm not saying that your decision was wrong. You've given yourself and your family a hard time, though. Flipping used cars is not the kind of job you deserve, and it definitely won't be able to make ends meet during wartime."

"Ensi was daydreaming about becoming the widow of a martyr, so she would be eligible for benefits. But she could have worked and contributed some money to the household instead. Am I wrong, Little Sis? I encouraged my wife to go to crochet classes, and I paid for them. Now that the kids go to school, she has enough time to crochet items to sell, rather than going to Quran reading sessions and chewing over and over that 1,400-year-old shit. She believes Haji's teaching that only men can be the providers for a family."

"Ah! Let Haji go to hell! Your wife says you always dump on her and her parents. She says you appear wearing only your boxers in front of your kids, tell jokes about Khomeini, and speak blasphemous words in private and public."

"Does she say anything about what she learns in her so-called Quran class?"

"What do you mean?"

"Ugh, she let slip that in the last lesson they discussed how there is no penalty for killing a *murtad*, an apostate."

"Bullshit!"

"Oh, yeah, that's why I'd rather speak my shitty mind than drivel on about barbarous crap, the belief in punishment by death for apostates in Islam. But now let's talk about good things, like Mati and little Nader."

"You might like to know that my baby, like his dead aunt, doesn't like to pee unless the toilet is sprayed with his father's *eau de cologne*."

"Ha ha! Remember I had to spray the old washroom with Maman Ashi's rose water to make it pleasant for Mati? What is the brand of your husband's *eau de cologne*? Maybe I'd better ask his son. But where is the baby?"

Via dell'Arco della Ciambella. To hide her anxiety about the evening dinner with Fari, Yalda busies herself hanging clothes in the closet, keeping half an eye on her son. He is sitting on the bottom edge of the bed in front of the open window. Leaning forward on his arms, his palms press on the unmade bed, he is shaking his legs as he looks outside. On the way from the airport to Fari's apartment, Nader, sitting in the back of the car and looking out the window, seemed calm and indifferent to their conversation about their halcyon schooldays.

That Fari almost ignored Nader at first might have made her son feel that way and thus seem well-behaved; however, Yalda felt upset and worried Fari wouldn't like her Little Bird. After all, she'd planned this trip to see if her old university classmate could be a father figure for her lonely son. Her big worry, though, is that Nader does not seem flexible enough to accept Fari as a father figure. Hanging up his new shirt and pants, she recalls how much they cost and calculates all the expenses for this trip in her head.

"It's cost me a lot," Yalda says under her breath.

Not expecting Nader to say anything, she keeps thinking. If her plan doesn't work, she will pay off her debts to Ali by washing more dishes in his restaurant and forcing herself to be deaf to Natalie's nagging. That's what she'll deserve, she thinks, if she fails to find a good father and a decent nest for her Little Bird, as well as a supportive man for herself.

"Oh, yeah! I won't hide the fact that I'm dying to work as an architect in Rome rather than as a dishwasher in Saint-Étienne," she says out loud. "This would be a good place for both of us, Little Bird, wouldn't it?"

Yalda turns back to Nader, but she doesn't see him on the bed. Looking around, she notices that the familiar view from the window has been replaced by the well-known corridor of Borromini with its forced perspective. Instead of the sculpture, she sees Nader at the end of the vista. She feels her cry dying in her throat, as the Gianicolo cannon shot rings in her head.

Via della Rosetta. With his mouth full of food, Fari is babbling about the market value of Persian rugs. Keeping one eye on the raw oysters disappearing into Fari's mouth, and the other eye on her own "oyster" who so far has been quiet and polite, Yalda is wondering how to change the subject so she can talk about her new plan. In order not to deviate from the purpose of her trip, she has to ignore Fari's greedy style of eating. She can't stand the smell of oysters, though. That her Little Bird also can't stand that smell of seafood either makes her even more worried. When Nader pushes his chair back to stand up, her eyes ask him where he is going. He replies by turning toward the washroom.

Letting out a sigh of relief, she turns to Fari, who is busy slurping and spitting out sentences embellished with French words. A gust of wind coming from the direction of the Pantheon sweeps down the street and she realizes Nader is missing. Running around the narrow streets surrounding the monument, out of the blue she notices that Lady Liaison is following her. For a moment, she doubts that she is in Rome. Lady Liaison, trying to catch her, shouts, "You cannot keep your kid in a vacuum forever." Yalda doesn't give a damn what she says. When Lady Liaison grabs her arm, she turns to face her. "Leave me alone! What do you want from me? My son and I aren't in Rasht anymore." Lady Liaison releases her arm to free her heel from the treacherous space between *sampietrini* and asks, "Is it a betrayal if I sleep with Piruz?" No way! Taking off her shoes, Lady Liaison asserts, "You never loved your husband, darling."

"Leave my son and me alone!"

"You've lost your son, Yalda."

Running into the temple, Yalda shouts, "Where the bloody hell are you, Nader?"

Rue du Cauchemar, the last dream. Palms and pines and planes and cypresses are turning and burning and tightening the circle around her Little Bird. Yalda musters her strength and tries to shout for help, but nothing comes out of her throat. Emerging from the ashes, she first finds herself right in the centre of the rotunda. Then she finds herself at the edge of a bed, on which a small body wrapped in a white sheet is shining in the dark. *Ou étais tu, mon petit oiseau?* She doesn't touch the body lest her Little Bird turn to ashes. She hears seagulls crying like babies. Yalda wonders why they are circling the Pantheon's dome at this time of night. Looking up, she sees all the coffers are occupied with the same cat, humping and hissing. In a sweat, she turns her face. The bed is empty. She feels the scream of seagulls echoing in her ears. In the presence of their sound, she hears the indistinct chit-chat of Lady Liaison and Fari. It seems to her that all of them are mocking her. Clutching the white sheet, she lies down on the bed and covers herself in the shroud. The oculus reveals a round patch of azure sky. For a moment, she sees an extraordinary bird made of pure light, flying away from her on stable wings.

27.

I HEAR MY HEARTBEAT IN MY EARS. *It proves that I am awake. I'm not going to open my eyes, though. I'm not going to get up to finish my woodle project unless you give me one more chance. No, I won't. Who knows? Maybe you will come back to me in my dreams. Can't you hear the beats? Not this pumpish lub-dub, lub-dub, but those wild beats of our crazy days. You will come to me in my dreams and listen to me, won't you? I don't want to subject you to sentimental words reminiscent of an old romance. I want to be naked before you. I have to do that before I leave you alone for good and let myself get lost in a sort of eccentric nirvana. Make fun of me, if you like, as I used to make fun of you when you talked about the new world order of your comrades. We both had doubts then; yours were about that rigid utopia of your leftist friends, and mine were about you. And still I have doubts, but this time they're about me, about whether I will bend or break, about whether I can put myself together again. The dead are free from doubts, I assume. So, why don't you come to me with your eyes wide open? Why don't you come to see how shattered I've become? Come to me with those brown eyes shining in that pale face! Ah! Stop coming to my dreams without eyes, without a face, my Nader!*

"My Nader." Hmm! How hollow it sounds! *Come to my dreams, please, just one more time, so that I can look into your eyes and say this phrase, "my Nader," is a lie. A lie that once sounded sweet. It poured from my lips to bring a smile to your face. A sweet childish lie! It's still sweet—sickly sweet. I still say it when you come to me. And when I catch myself in this lie, I justify it by saying that I just use it to differentiate between you and the other Nader, the one who terrifies me now—he is still a closed book to me, despite having grown inside me.*

Ah! Let me keep my eyes closed! The world feels like it's closing in from all sides. I have no interest in such a world. I want to sink into your eyes. I want to tell you that you were a closed book to me, too—not a horrifying one, though. A book on my shelf; a book that was to be an absolute joy to read; a book that I always thought would open itself up to me as we lived our lives together. Goodness, how naïve I was!

Behind my eyelids, I let hordes of clouds come and go. Then a sea of yellow flowers emerges under an intact azure dome of the sky. Wow, what a lovely May day! And in a moment you will appear in front of me, somewhere between the sea of yellow flowers and the sky. I will see you in your pure white shirt with your hands folded behind your back, and your entire body hanging in the air. But you were shot, I will shout, with your eyes open and shining in your pale face. Above your body, I will see only a dark blindfold, but not your face, or your eyes. I want to see your face, I will cry, and your eyes, my Nader.

I hear an abrupt thunderclap. I shut up, finding myself lying on the usual bench. Our bench is under a weeping willow; leaden raindrops fall on my face. A familiar pain lodged in my lower back surprises me. I know I'm not awake. I want to sit up and look around for my Nader. There is nothing here but the wide plain, blemished with blood, and the sky, saturated with smog.

Frightened, Yalda opens her eyes to the rented den.

The mellow grey light of dawn, coming in through the small window, reaches the shadow man's bed and proclaims that some time has passed. She feels something warm and slippery appear between her legs. Not a good time to come back, she thinks, becoming fully alert. It's been a while since she stopped carrying pads, even though she knew it was not over. Perimenopause, although as unwanted a guest as the period itself, has so far been subtle enough that she has been able to ignore it during the chaos of the past year. With thighs pressed together to avoid leakage, she gets up and drags herself to the bathroom.

Under a low-pressure but hot shower, she lifts her face and lets her eyes and skin be sprayed with water. The soothing touch of water droplets reminds her how thirsty her skin is for a caress. It's not the right time to notice it, she thinks. Not now, when she has no one. She is not among those women who think this natural change of life is a catastrophe. Or, if this part sucks, it does as much as the beginning. It's just one of a zillion imperfections that one is supposed to bear. Being realistic, though, doesn't mean she does not desire a loving touch, or even more than that, the touch of a lover. Or even much more than that, the touch of a lover like her Nader—not perfect, but passionate. Not a Gregory Peck, but an honest lover. Piruz, although he had little passion, was also honest, she has to admit. She reflects. He was not honest so much as frank—frank enough to not hide the fact that he only loved himself. But who knows? Maybe nothing was wrong with him and his ego. Maybe she couldn't be happy with Piruz because she was always comparing him unfavourably with her Nader. Yalda has no doubt that if her Nader had survived, their romance wouldn't have lasted. While he was in jail, she dated Piruz because she needed somebody to keep her company. But it turned out that Piruz was more than "somebody."

Like a praying Shia, she raises her hands before her face and fixes her eyes on her palms, collecting droplets in their furrows. When she has a bit of water in her hands, she lets it slip through her fingers. As if she is performing ablution, she touches her face with her clean hands. Then her hands, turning heretical, slide down over her neck, breasts, tummy, and thighs, where a thin rivulet of blood mixing with water runs down her legs to vanish into the drain.

Sitting on the edge of the bed uneasily, she wonders what she can use for a sanitary pad. She glances at her watch. Too early to go out, she thinks. She pulls forward the old leather suitcase lying beside the bed. Grabbing a cotton T-shirt, she digs the eyebrow scissors out of her purse. As she lays the T-shirt flat on the bed to cut the sleeves and shape it into a napkin, her minds flies to her Nader's dorm room, where she used to visit him in secret. Whenever he took a break from his easel, he would sit on the only chair. She would sit, legs crossed or with arms around knees, on his single bed to watch him, babbling about everything and nothing.

"Look, Nader. I have a story for you. Shall I tell it or not?"

"Um…."

"No, seriously. I'm not kidding! It's funny but maybe a bit embarrassing. Promise you won't give me a dirty look when I tell you."

"Okay."

"Good! You know, if it had not been a girly story, I might have told it to my Dadashi to make him laugh. Things have changed, though, and we've lost the intimacy we had when were children."

"Aha!"

"Well, let me tell you the story. You know how Dadash Yunes and I feel about my nephew, Kami, Sister Eti's spoiled son?"

"Are you talking about the guy who's going to get a job in SAVAK?"

"Yes, but it's not SAVAK. It's the office of the prime minister."

"Doesn't make a difference."

"Come on, Nader. Don't be a tough commie!"

"We're living in a land where the king is considered the shadow of God. I wish I were a subversive commie instead of an art student."

"Fair enough. But back to my anecdote. I bet it'll make you smile."

"Really?"

"Oh, yeah! I was home alone. It was after Maman Ashi's death, and I was living in Sister Eti's house. She was out. I don't remember whether she was at a party or shopping. Most of the time, I refused to go out with her. I was extremely stubborn at that age."

"Where were the men of the house?"

"I don't remember. It was summertime and nobody liked to stay home. I loved it because I could do whatever I liked."

"Like what? Dancing?"

"Oh, no. You know I'm not a dance person. I was drawing, doodling in fact, while listening to a tape, the latest gift from Dadash Yunes, and daydreaming. I was having a good time, and then I noticed that I had started my period."

"Ahem!"

"Don't be a prude, Nader! What's wrong with a damn period?"

"All right! Keep telling the story!"

"Well, I had no pads at home, even though Sister Eti had always told me to have some on hand. I searched all her drawers and couldn't find anything. Pretty helpless, I found a brand new white cotton T-shirt in Kami's drawer, which was always full of new, never-worn stuff. Now you can guess what I did."

"What?"

"Well, I had no choice. It was better and safer than making a sanitary napkin from one of his father's shirts. He was obsessed with clothes!"

"So innovative!"

Not at all, she thinks, as she throws away the extra pieces of fabric. She recalls she forced herself not to tell him that the credit for the invention really belonged to her brother—but that was another story. Dadashi had come up with the idea when he cut a brand new white sheet to make a handkerchief for Mati. It was one of his many pranks. She had no clue if her Nader would find this hilarious, though. She didn't want to give him the wrong impression of her brother.

She tries the homemade pad. It will be good for a couple of hours so that she can take her time before leaving the house. At another time, an unexpected period would have ruined her day. Now, like a host who knows the guest is about to leave, she feels hospitable. She wants a cup of borage tea to ease her back pain, but she settles for thyme tea, the only kind she has.

With her favourite throw—knitted and gifted by Afi—over her shoulders, and a mug crowned with dancing vapours in her hand, she kneels down beside the altar. The white paper on the top of the pile of her woodles is titled "Nader." Yalda rests her mug on the table and picks up her pencil. Adding a "my" before the title, she begins to sketch.

28.

AH, WHAT A RELIEF, MY NADER! *We've left behind not only the narrow streets of downtown Montreal, but also the busy Route Transcanadienne and that damned, deceiving Toronto turn-off. Honestly, I still doubt I've completely suppressed the anguish I feel as a mother of an estranged son. I can admit that, an hour ago, when I was hanging out in the mall, I felt a craving for Nader and immediately tried to convince myself that it was a craving for you. Three months ago, in a cab in downtown Toronto, it occurred to me that the only way to escape hell was to go on a quest for a self-defined nirvana. Now, I would like to give you a ride down the mountain—not one of those gorgeous mountains of the Alborz, The Dome of the World,* mais un petit mont du Québec. *Nonetheless, since I picked Rigaud as our destination, I began to feel worry creeping into my mind. I was afraid that my motherly instinct would make me turn the steering wheel towards the Toronto rather than Ottawa. You see how pathetic I am? One moment I'm wishing my son would die and relieve me of my misery, and the next I'm dying to see my son, no matter what!*

Now, let me take a gulp of my coffee before it gets tepid. Yummy. Isn't coffee a heavenly drink? I feel as if heaven is just a mile away. I am driving on a quiet winter road with snow-covered landscapes passing by and my beloved Nader beside me. What a great plan! I'm proud of myself for coming up with it. One more thing we need is music. You don't mind if I start with my favourite, "The Fountain," do you? I bet if you were still alive, you would have put it on your top ten list—even above Bartok and Satie. Yeah, let's begin with "Stay with Me." Then it goes to "Tree of Life." We're not going to live together forever in Eden, though. Hm! We couldn't even live together in hell! And then, it's "Death is the Road to Awe," which I love the most. Oh, don't tell me not to babble while listening to music! When I lived with other living people, I always bit my tongue while listening to music. Living with the dead necessitates different rules, my dear. Furthermore, my babbling is a soundtrack that fills your silence. Let me keep gabbing to you, for I never tell you enough when you visit me in my dreams.

Where do I go from here, though? Where is my silver horse taking us? Perhaps we will come to a cliff and find Vishnu sitting heavily on a stone, stretching out one of his arms to remove this damned burden from me. Or are we just heading to the end of the road? After all, horses should know better than us which road goes to nirvana—is it the one that passes through this modest Quebec mountain, or the one that pierces through the wild heart of an exotic place like Mumbai or Machu Picchu? Or is it the road that leads to Toronto? The dead should know as well. But you won't know how to get there until you get there, right? And I know you're not going to speak to me when I'm awake. Yeah, I'd better leave the directions to my horse and concentrate on figuring out what nirvana is. Is it a specific state of mind, a state of body, or both? I don't know. I feel dumb. But I sense I'm on my way to it. Believe it or not, I didn't choose it; it chose me. Like a mule, I have been carrying my burden along this road of life. And then I encountered the final bang in my head—not just because I learned my Little Bird is going to be an armed guard for armoured vans that transport money, but because I learned that the son I raised and love hates me. Ah! What could be worse than planting love and harvesting hatred? You see, I have no way out other than keeping my face towards nirvana so that all my shadows fall behind me. That's not enough, though. I know. Perhaps no shadows fall in nirvana. Well, we'll see.

Voilà! Raindrops dabbing the windshield! No reason to worry about anything, my dear. Trust my old horse! I caress the supple neck of my horse, not the solid steering wheel. Yeah, my horse knows the way. And I have no choice but to keep going until the end. No, he won't leave me alone in the middle of the road—unlike what you and your namesake did to me.

Not a complaint at all! Don't take offence, my Nader. How can I blame you for running to an untimely death? Your death is the reason that I've been able to keep you to myself in my dreams. Over all these years, whenever I felt your loss was too much for me to bear, I reminded myself that if you had lived, our relationship would have ended. Instead, you remain a lover for all seasons. I cannot even blame your namesake, the second fugitive Nader, who denied me and all that I did in my life. No, I can't do that. I have no ruler in hand to measure anybody. And so, I can hardly blame myself. Everybody moves in their own orbit. Don't ask me why! You believed in free will and I tried to do the same. You didn't die a hero's death at all. And I, fleeing from the will of others, became an ungodly wanderer. Hmm, isn't it repayment for my rebellion against destiny?

Yeah, laugh at me if you like. I don't mind. See how my only working wiper dances on the rain-dappled windshield? Is that a curse too? Endlessly, it approaches the other wiper, and then endlessly steps back from it. When I got close to the turn-off for Toronto, I avoided it. But it's not because I wanted to hold onto my pride or to stick to my values, as he had said. After all, what would be the point of coming back to a son who is determined to refute me? You judge, my Nader! What I'm saying is simple. Nader's future can go one of two ways: he will shoot or he will be shot—at least potentially. But our choices are all about potentiality. As the woman who gave him life, how can

I not take the worst-case scenario into account? Remember our long discussions on this topic? You always defended the beliefs of your political friends, and I was not smart enough to beat you in an argument, but my heart assured me I was right to deny them, to deny any value, any act, any goal that could take you away from me. You never used a gun, but you were shot because you justified the use of one under "certain circumstances." And it drove me crazy when your namesake also used this phrase—"certain circumstances"—in his argument. Well, maybe I'm just a fucking fanatic when it comes to guns, but at least I don't have a heart made of stone. I can't accept my loved ones putting themselves in danger.

Yuck! Again a dry mouth! I wish I could drink the raindrops instead of this lukewarm coffee. I'm glad my eyes are dry, though. They are as cold as bullets before being fired. December rain in Quebec is so different from May showers in Tehran. Believe it or not, my eyes were springs after I lost you, when I began my forty-day period of mourning. They were always full of tears during my Lent-like seclusion. You didn't come to my disturbed dreams then; my only witness was the jinn, the only one who grieved with me during those crazy nights. God knows what could have stopped my crying if Afi hadn't appeared to bring me a message from you on the fortieth day. When she left, my eyes felt rested and soothed. It's true that I had already made up a story in my mind, but it was vague. In it, my beloved was in a disgusting dungeon, subjected to intolerable torture. That was all I had in my head. The execution refused to take shape in my mind. Afi filled in the details; she made me replace what I imagined with her version of events, which sounded more alive and authentic. Did she spill the beans about her girlish love for you then? No, not at all. That was years later, when she gave me the throw she had knitted for you, the one that is now draped over the back of the car seat. You see how nice it is! I really love its burgundy and charcoal stripes. The one she'd knitted for her brother was plain. I guess you saw it in jail. When she insisted on giving it to me as a souvenir, I wondered why she hadn't asked Ali to pass it on to you. She later told me that at first, the idea of knitting a throw for her brother and his prison-mate seemed like a good one. But then she worried that the gesture would somehow disclose her feelings for you—maybe because this throw was nicer than the one she'd made for Ali. In Saint-Étienne, I used to boast that my throw was far better than Ali's. I never told Ali about his sister's secret, though. To tell the truth, I didn't want to accept the gift, but Afi convinced me. She told me that the reason she didn't offer it to you was not just because she was too shy. She felt she had no right to nourish a childish love for a stranger who was in love with someone else. I cannot understand the logic behind these words. You know, she's a "simple perfect woman," just like the ones that our favourite poet, Forough, describes. You see, my Nader, you chose such a woman, unknowingly, to bring me a message from you. She came to me too late—forty days after I'd heard the news. Nonetheless, Afi acted as my saviour by telling me some of the things you had said and giving me some details about the prison. She also described your execution; she told me a glorious story of a brave hero of oppressed people who kept his head up and his eyes open before the firing squad. After she left my sombre room, I felt like I could see the sun again. It was a gentle sun, reflecting in the eyes of a man with no regrets.

Ouch! This nerve pain in my back is killing me, my Nader. I can imagine when you were in jail you felt miserable, as if the little mouse of fear was chewing off pieces of you bit by bit. What you must have felt at the moment you were shot in the back was different, though. While I listened to Ali's version of events, I wondered what the difference was between one single shot in the back and numerous shots coming right before your eyes. Was that the difference between a hero and a coward? You were too smart to make yourself into an example of a political hero. I don't remember why

Ali told me about that. It was one of those wintery Sunday afternoons when there was nothing for us to do but drive out of town. Natalie was busy with her church friends, and my Little Bird was restless to go out. In the morning, he'd given me your letters, saying that at first you'd wanted to send them from jail along with your picture. Apparently, you changed your mind at the last minute, saying you would be free soon. When I finally read them, I saw that your letters didn't show any hope at all. While those few old, wrinkled papers rested in my hands, I expected to read run-of-the-mill love letters. Instead, they were short notes addressed to a vague person, reflecting your horror and your doubts. You were very much afraid of having insufficient physical stamina against torture and putting your comrades at risk, of writing a false confession letter and wounding your pride, of betraying your friends, and, of course, of an untimely death. My fingers trembled as I held the papers, feeling the wavering flow of confusion beneath your words. It made me suddenly angry with myself for thinking of you as a Superman—not to mention a Romeo—rather than a fragile and changeable man. You see, my Nader, I was such an obnoxiously naïve girl! Once little Nader was asleep in the backseat—wrapped tightly in both of Afi's throws—Ali hesitantly began to talk. His hesitation probably came from not knowing whether to uphold or shatter my false image of you as an idol. You don't think I was shocked to hear his version of the story, do you? Now, we are far from the days of those perfect heroes, from the time of a painful revolution that shook the seemingly solid ground beneath our feeble feet.

Ah! The rain falls down on us but doesn't wash away our wounds. Tell me, my Nader, why is this so? One winter day, a long time ago now, in the Saint-Étienne suburbs, I was listening to a new version of the story emerge from under Ali's drooping moustache and longing for a heavy rain to compensate for my tearless eyes. At the same time as I was listening to Ali's story,

I was hearing a voice in my head already retelling the story. By no means could I have guessed that Nader had a plan. So, my Nader planned his own death in order to not be surprised by his executioners. Although Nader was not allowed to have visitors, he was out of solitary confinement, which was a good sign. Yet my Nader was afraid. I had never understood why Nader had made friends with one of his boorish, teenage guards; despite his shyness, he was still a guard. So, my Nader chose a good guy to be his angel of death. I had thought Nader was trying to get the guy on our side. But no, my Nader knew it wouldn't do any good to preach a new world order to a young bumpkin who had become a revolutionary guard through the easily accessible channel of a local mosque. Instead, Nader persuaded him to be dutiful in his job as an armed guard. My Nader fooled that poor boy into doing what he could not do himself. It was not possible for Nader to commit suicide in jail—he was never alone, and there were no sharp objects available. But it was easy for my Nader to push a newly hired guard with a gun to shoot a single bullet at a prisoner who dared to flee right in front of his eyes. Nader wanted to die before he did anything wrong. And, in the end, my Nader succeeded in getting out of hell by making a murderer of an innocent young man....

Oh, what a shame to judge you so harshly, my Nader! You wanted to die because you could not trust yourself. And then it was the same story with me. You didn't give that boy a gun, but you pushed him to pull the trigger. And I didn't give my boy a gun, but I pushed him out into a world where it is normal to pull the trigger, a world that operates by "survival of the fittest." Remember I never liked this term? I found its central idea unfair. I discussed this with you when you encouraged me to study those so-called "white cover" books, which were banned for their subversive themes. Do you know what happened to them? You always said they were your only treasure. Shortly after your arrest, I buried them in the backyard's small flowerbed with Dadash Yunes's help. It was before I moved out of that little old house, the house where we had the brief joy of living together.

Well, you see, once again, we're together—far from the fucking crowd, and stripped of any bravado. No hero, no winner—what a well-matched couple we are! What could be better than this? You're with me and I'm riding my horse to our "Road to Awe." Look! It's up there! Watch the snow-covered hill through the curtain of rain. Let me turn off "The Fountain" and stop along the shoulder of the road. Now, here we are, the two of us, face to face with the cliff. Isn't it gorgeous? But why don't you show me your face, my Nader, while we're not in a dream?

29.

TO SHAKE THE DOUBTS FROM HER MIND, Yalda steps away from the red mailbox and sits down on the free corner of a bench in the middle of the mall. She digs an unfinished letter out of her bag. This morning, just before leaving the studio, she found it by chance and hesitated before throwing it away.

No help wanted, no help offered, she thinks, letting her eyes run over the lines. She had written them right after her arrival in Montreal.

Piruz,

You're smart enough to imagine how difficult it is for me to ask you for help after being out of touch for so long. It's hard to accept defeat and express it to someone who's already denied you the right to prove yourself. Well, you won the bet. I failed. Go ahead and curse me for my failure as a single mother. What is harder, though, is that I have no hope of rebuilding the broken bridge between you and Nader. When once I was assertive, I now feel helpless. That my estranged son has no real friends or loving family in such a crappy world scares me to death. And that he hates me, that he believes I've ruined his life, prevents me from supporting him. I won't blame you if you reject my request. I admit that I deprived you of seeing your son. I only told you that Nader and I would be visiting Sister Eti in Essen; I didn't tell you that we would never come back. No wonder you think that I fooled you, that I betrayed you, that I stole Nader from you. When I called you from Essen to let you know I wouldn't be coming back to a place where my rights as a mother were denied, I wanted to explain, if not excuse myself. You refused to hear what I had to say: that my only chance to protect my rights was to deny yours, that I couldn't stand the living in the country or at home, and that the double standard in your attitude was beyond what I had expected. On the one hand, you refuted Sharia, but on the other you held onto it, either to have the upper hand with me, or to justify qisas *in the case of my brother's murder—an eye for an eye. When I called, you refused to hear my voice. You reminded me that you would not have any responsibility for Nader anymore. Remember I called you some years later, from Montreal? I thought then that an absent father was better than no father for a lonely, depressed teenager. I begged you to call Nader and break the ice, but you ignored my message. I doubt you did that because you could not forgive me, and it's hard to believe you're resentful enough to punish Nader for what I did. Rather, I assume you rejected my call simply because you'd already erased both of us from your mind. So, why am I still...?*

No point in asking for help for an obviously confused boy from a man who only cares about himself, she thinks. She stands up to find a trash bin, crumpling up the letter in her fist.

She steps into the supermarket with its bright lights and shiny floors and then pauses, wondering how she ended up there. She has a few minor errands to do during her last day in Montreal, including buying some groceries to fill the shadow man's small fridge. But it'd be better to do this one at the end of the day—not just because it's common sense, but because it's better to put off doing what she doesn't like to do. Shopping at a supermarket is annoying for a person who hates shopping. She doesn't mind going to the outdoor *marché*, but it's out of question on a late December day. She'll rush to a depanneur and grab something before heading back to the subletted den at the end of the day.

So, why am I here? Yalda thinks. Perhaps her quest for nirvana has brought her here. Since she came up with the idea to go on this journey *à la mode de chez elle*, she's been trying to follow where her unconscious mind leads her in the hope of unravelling either the awful mystery of the ruined relations between her and her son, or the dilemma of her awkward life. She is not unhappy with this compliance. It seems as though her ego finds yielding to herself more comfortable than yielding to the authority of others.

Because of this new resolution, the store is just one place among many that she's visited like a sleepwalker in the city— routes and *rues*, *quartiers* and parks, bars and cafés, schools and offices. With her senses on high alert for traces of a lost past, she is still looking for the missing link.

"Goodness! Where and when did he become a brick wall to me?" she mutters.

Either by instinct or intelligence, she's concluded that her relationship with Nader changed when they lived in Montreal; it was there that their connection had been lost, as though the cord had been severed. Now she wonders if there was ever a thread at all.

"Ridiculous!" she says aloud.

For twenty years, nothing could crack her stupid belief that her son was, if not in and of her being, at least a representation of it.

"Now I can imagine how the fucking non-existent God got frustrated with what he produced," she says to herself.

An imbecile like her deserved a bang on the head; she needed to open her eyes and see she was not the soil and he was not a plant. The last thing she ever wanted for him was to be involved in violence, and he was choosing a job that put him right in the line of fire. If she hadn't discovered his secret, she would have kept wrapping her son up in her illusions forever.

Yalda shakes her head, returning to the here and now. In order not to look like a shoplifter, she picks up a basket and starts walking along the aisles, her eyes passing over the brands and tags. She is sure there is a surveillance camera, if not a store detective, watching for people who look confused or distracted—the primary giveaway of a shoplifter. Yet not all suspects are neophytes. And not all neophytes look suspicious.

The only item she considers throwing into her basket is a pack of chewing gum from the display next to the cash register. But she doesn't reach for it as she doesn't intend to leave right away. She likes to linger around the store where she shoplifted for the first and last time. It was during their first year in a city that had offered her nothing other than a touch of French. With all her savings spent on rent and private school tuition, she was facing the matter of daily survival, a struggle she kept hidden from her eleven-year-old son. She never shoplifted again, not because she was ashamed of herself for stealing food to feed their hungry tummies, but because she was too much of a coward to keep doing it. Shortly afterwards, she was lucky enough to get a job in a bakery, where she burned her hands rather than her soul.

The supermarket is not just a crime scene, though, Yalda thinks, dragging her feet on the slippery floor as she makes her way towards the frozen food section. It's also where she bought high-quality frozen shrimp for Nader a couple of years later, after getting the job offer for the project in Springfield. Suddenly it occurs to her that the Springfield stage was a turning point. Unable to convince Nader to accept another move and desperate to resolve the disagreement, she decided to let him stay in Montreal while she travelled back and forth. She wanted the new job not only for the occasional indulgence like shrimp for Nader and perfume for herself, but also to regain part, if not all, of the dignity she'd lost over the years of taking jobs just to get by. And soon Marc, a potential love interest, appeared on the scene, making her even happier about her decision. In the end, those challenging days of hard work and commuting brought her nothing more than some money, the bitter aftertaste of a sudden but inevitable breakup with Marc, and an iron curtain between her and Nader.

At the time, she hadn't thought that her job at Springfield could destroy her relationship with her son. Feeling a quick chill, she steps quickly into another aisle, away from the freezers. She admitted that, in the back of her mind, she felt a bit guilty for letting Mark into her life for a while. It was unavoidable, though—for the first time since leaving Tehran, she had enough money and "me time" to think about finding love for herself, rather than just a substitute father for her son. For better or worse, inviting Mark into her heart infringed on the space Nader had always taken up there. On the other hand, in her right mind, she did not believe at all in the traditional image of mother who sacrifices anything and everything for her child. As she tried to balance being the perfect mom with being a happy woman, her newfound confidence led her to underestimate the curtain she could feel but did not want to see.

In the cereal aisle, Yalda browses the shelves involuntarily to see if Nader's favourite cereal, Honey Smacks, is available. In the time of the cold war between a baffled mom and a flaky teenage boy with a cracking voice and oily skin, she kept buying it in the hope that the frog mascot would bring a smile to his face or a sweet word to his lips, as it used to do when he was a little kid. It turned out that neither the silly-looking frog nor the trendy Xbox were able to work a miracle. As things got hellish and he suddenly refused to go to school, it seemed to Yalda that her son, consumed by his video games, was invincible. She couldn't reach him. She forced herself to swallow her pride and call Piruz to ask for help. He proved to be as impenetrable as his son. Just when she was sinking into total helplessness, fate gave her a helping hand: Nader put up with the idea of moving back to Toronto, where he could go to a public English school and she could get a new contract job as a drafter, thanks to her fresh American experience.

"Maybe I was not grateful enough to the invisible hand of fate to avoid its accusing finger," she whispers, taking her eyes off the frog that was not capable of being her accomplice.

With an empty basket in her hand, swaying back and forth, she moves towards the cash register. A woman with rounded shoulders walking in front of her catches her eye. Dressed in all black, she is moving with heavy steps. Yalda pauses. The woman looks exactly like Rima. Although it is no wonder to come across women in Montreal who look like her student, she feels her heartbeat accelerating. She pictures Rima's face, remembering that the poor mother is now wandering through the cursed land—the one that houses the Abu-Ghraib prison—in search of her son.

"Oh, Rima," she murmurs, fixing her eyes on the woman's back, "I imagine how you must be feeling."

When the woman reaches the end of the aisle, Yalda can see her face—she has the same tawny complexion, but not the same pale smile and expressive eyes. She sighs, wondering how her failures as a mother compare to Rima's.

Rima failed to teach her son not to infect his wounds with vengeance, she thinks. Yet all hope is not lost yet for her—as long as her son's love for her hasn't turned to hate. Yalda notices her mouth and throat are dry. She tries to produce some saliva to swallow. Instead, a lump of grief goes down her throat. She doesn't think Rima is guilty at all, but her head is full of doubt about herself. Wasn't she too ignorant, too busy, too overwhelmed, too fucking blind? Didn't she teach Nader to value human life and dignity over the rules and orders of any hierarchy?

"Or maybe I was a bad role model for him because I overvalued individual free will and responsibility," she thinks, returning her empty basket to its place and leaving the supermarket.

The department store, unlike the supermarket, is pleasantly warm and bright. It will put her in a better mood before the final round of her trip. She takes off her long, hooded jacket and crams it into a shopping bag so she can move around more easily. She's not planning on trying on any clothes, but she still needs free hands.
"Rima, you look really nice today."
"Thank you.... I just got this ... outfit ... the other day."
"Really. Where did you get it?"
"I got it from ... from Macy's."
"Teacher, we don't have Macy's here."
"Nandita, please wait your turn!"
"Sorry, teacher. Where do you get your outfit?"
"Ah, silly brain, stop singing the same old song! I'm not going back to a dead-end past," she says to herself, still hearing the fading echo of Nandita's voice.
"Where do you get your outfit, teacher?"
Nandita cannot be quiet until she gets a response, she thinks. Well, Yalda didn't get her outfit from Macy's, or from any other department store. When it comes to shopping, a department store is no better than a supermarket. It may even be a bit more boring—unlike a supermarket, it doesn't inspire any urge to shoplift, even in the manner of Robin Hood.
It has another kind of appeal, though. Yalda stands in front of a mirror and stares at the pathetic face of a scrawny woman. She has a scar on her shaved head and sad smile lines around her open mouth.
"Send in the clowns, poor woman!" she says, making a face at the mirror and turning to the escalator.
In a department store, the escalator is the number one way to cheer yourself up, Yalda thinks. It is one of her oldest tricks. It always reminds her of the sweet awe she felt the first time

she tried it in the Ferdowsi Department Store, the first one in Tehran. All her trips to the store, escorted by Big Brain and Big Heart, were fun. She remembered watching Mati try on stylish dresses and pose in front of the mirror, Dadashi misplacing items craftily, and the whole gang licking a vanilla ice cream cone or blowing pink bubble gum while riding up and down the escalator. They were all so happy. Years later, in one of those boring trips to the store with Sister Eti and Maman Ashi, she argued with Sister Eti about those happy days.

Maman Ashi had noticed a Sleeping Beauty-like mannequin that reminded her of Mati. Remembering her lost daughter, she could not help her tears. And Sister Eti had revealed her bias against Mati: "She would have eaten mouse poison if she hadn't died of consumption. Such a melancholic girl was Mati, Maman."

"It's all bullshit, Sister Eti!" Yalda screamed.

Maybe there was a bit of truth in Sister Eti's words, Yalda thinks now. Nevertheless Mati, a real free spirit, was capable of laughing in some of the rare moments when she was not bothered by people and things she didn't like. But without a doubt, a braggart like Sister Eti, and all maladors, bothered her a lot.

Riding an escalator seems childish now, but sampling a pleasing scent in the cosmetics section still cheers her up. Not in the mood to chat, she avoids eye contact with the busy assistants. Browsing the perfume testers, she hesitates, unsure which to choose. After a pause, she tries Arpege for her right wrist and Shalimar for her left. Taking a deep breath, she moves on to her next trick for cheering herself up. She knows a no-cost method to make herself into a Hollywood Cleopatra. It requires a sort of crassness that would not be endorsed by her refined sister, though. Yalda shrugs her shoulders and begins by dabbing tinted moisturizer onto her face, patting it over her hollow cheeks.

"Mati's short life, despite its sad end, was decent—not shitty." Yalda repeats what she once said to Sister Eti, when they were living together in Essen. The eldest sibling insisted again, though not with her old assertiveness, that Mati was born depressed. Yalda knew what was behind Sister Eti's words: Mati's father, a humble but handsome *setar* player who lost his life to alcohol, left only one thing for his daughter: depression. Yalda's father, although still not a stepfather that Sister Eti could boast about, was a better choice. He didn't bring any disgrace to "our prestigious family." Furthermore, he left a fortune. It gradually and secretly slipped into the hands of Sister Eti's husband, only to be lost in dubious bad investments.

Mati was luckier than Dadash Yunes and me for not living long enough to be drowned in a sea of crap, she thinks. It's true, though, that Mati was inclined to become sick at heart by the banal minutia of life. As she looks for a lipstick that can add some colour to her dismal life, her brain tries to figure out what is responsible for depression—genes or environment? Whichever it is, what matters is that her sister, long dead, was not the only one in the family whose life was coloured by melancholy. Yalda used to console herself about seeing her son so down in the dumps by telling herself that it wasn't a big deal, that it ran in the family. It comes and goes like mould in the house, she would say.

"*Et enfin*, your hope bubble burst, baby!" she says under her breath. She chooses a rosy lipstick and rubs it on forcefully, as if coating and covering mould stains on a ruined wall.

Out of the mall and away from the bustling holiday atmosphere, she stops to heave a long sigh. She needs a few minutes to understand time and place: December, Montreal. This evening is going to be "Yalda Eve," the longest night of the year; it is not only the Persian winter solstice celebration, but also her half-century mark. In addition, the city is under the spell of *Noël*. But Montreal is not the same as it was before, when she was happy to buy Persian Delight along with *Bûche de Noël* for her beloved son. It's now showing its harsh side. Since last October, when she happened to listen to *that murderer's mother* on the air, Montreal has become the hometown of a mother who's gone through an *'orrible* ordeal. And on top of it, this cold city is now where Yalda must cast away all the shadows of her life, especially her shadow son.

Her eyes wander, and for a moment she imagines herself approaching passersby with a made-up face, asking, "Pardon, do you know how it feels when your son sees you as a fucking nightmare?"

Yalda feels her lungs filling up with frigid air. The clouds, hanging low over the tops of buildings, catch her eye. Snow is on the way, she thinks, closing her eyes, hoping to shift gears.

Now, where do I go from here, Madame? *Au cimetière?*

In fact, the idea of visiting the cemetery popped into her mind as soon as she arrived in Montreal. She hasn't crossed it off her list yet. As she wandered the streets of the city, there were moments when she thought the cemetery was a must-see place. After all, it was the work of a well-known landscape designer, and it was one of the first places she'd visited ten years ago, when she'd first arrived in the city. Then, she'd been fueled by the idea of establishing herself in her career and in a new home, and making a sunny future for her son.

"At this time of year, it's not the rural cemetery whose robins and hawthorns I once adored," she says to herself, "it's just a frozen city of the dead overlooking the mess of the living."

Whatever it is, she just can't stop herself from going to visit the place where evil sleeps beside good. She feels the urge to go up there and find graves covered by the cruel whiteness of snow.

She opens her eyes and sees a falling curtain of snow dividing her from the street, jammed with cars, and the sidewalk, packed with pedestrians. After casting a doubtful glance at her old leather boots, she thrusts her purse under her jacket and tightens the strings of her hood. As she steps forward, she spots a woman in the crowd toddling along the icy sidewalk. Fixing her eyes on the woman's black umbrella and her drooping shoulders, Yalda takes a deep breath and advances towards *Chemin de la Forêt*.

30.

YALDA MOVES HER HEAD TO GET OUT OF THE DREAM. She opens her eyes to the cell, takes her head off the altar and her hand off the pile of woodles. Under the light of the old-fashioned bulb, everything around her looks organized. Her bags, all packed, are placed beside the door, indicating the end of her stay. Nonetheless, Yalda Eve is dragging on.

Not a big deal, she thinks. She's going to get up, brush her teeth, empty her bladder, replace the sharp yellowish light with a dim reddish one, and go to the shadow man's bed to rest.

But before going back to sleep, Yalda wants to ruminate on her dream.

It had a prelude, an impertinent single image that appeared for a second and vanished. Like a picture in an old album, it looked motionless: she was sitting somewhere, a cozy room, maybe with legs under the quilt covering a *korsi*, a stool-like frame of wood that is set up above a fire. Her son was beside her, leaning his small head against her big arm. They didn't look happy or sad, just relaxed and calm. Then the dream began—full, clear, moving, and meaningful. She was on a small boat, standing upright with a paddle in each hand, looking ahead. She was not paddling—the boat was surfing forward, smoothly and steadily, on the water with tiny gentle tides. She had the feeling that she was on the Persian Gulf, although she has never been there before. The water in the south, based on the pictures and movies she has seen, should be crystal blue, shining with a Mediterranean kind of colour. It was not. A dull greenish grey, it could have been the Karun River—as unknown to her as the Persian Gulf. Or it could have been the Saint Lawrence, the only river that was familiar to her. Strangely, she had no fear of the water. Before falling asleep, while going over her woodles, she'd wished to have a flying dream—a kind of a birthday wish for herself. There were times in the past when she could have one whenever she had a hunger for it. This time, for whatever reason, flying yielded to sailing. Although it was neither familiar nor inspiring to her in any way, it was not frightening. As long as there was a boat between her feet and the water, she felt safe. And she was not alone. Before fixing her eyes straight ahead, she spotted a man sitting at the back of the boat. It was Yunes, but he didn't look very welcoming, as he usually did when he met with his beloved little sister. He was sad and silent, and somehow she knew he was dead. Focused on the shore, which was still hidden from her sight, and the water surrounding the boat, she felt no need to ask him anything. That he was with her in his afterlife was not disturbing, but rather reassuring—just as he had always been when they were children. She was aware, though, that as a visitor coming from the world of the dead, he would have no hand in this world. When the boat approached the shoreline, a deconstructivist building came into view. Erected in an empty space, it was like a huge natural beehive with enormous cells, each occupied by clergy students of Qom seminary schools—male students in turbans and robes, and female ones in black *chador*. Wondering where she was, she spotted Ensi and her older daughter, Turan, in one of the cells. Then, when she turned around to speak to Yunes, she found Piruz in his place. His back was to her, and he had paddles in his hands. "Where is Yunes?" she asked.

"At the bottom of the deep sea—far away from you, who betrayed your brother, Yalda."

"Bullshit!"

"You held the hand of his lying son, Yalda. It turned out that he had been involved in the murder of his father."

"You tell me, Piruz, how could I let a teenage boy stay in jail?"

"You allowed your brother's wife and his twins to fulfill their plan by forgoing your right to equal retaliation, to *qisas*. And because you gave your nephew a chance to pardon his accomplices, the sentence they received was the very minimum."

"How the hell do you expect me to accept this right to *qisas*, when I don't believe in it?"

"Huh, how could you keep your mouth shut, Yalda, when the victim was your own brother? Little wonder in a land under Sharia, a super smart and fanatical woman plotted the murder of her husband who'd turned his back on both Islam and his wife!"

She opened her mouth to say something to Piruz, but it filled with water and pulled her down into the dark depths of sleep.

Why the heck are you back in my dream, Dadash Yunes?

It's Yalda Eve, and I want to tell you the tale of my little sis's birth.

Ah! I'd rather hear the tale of a brother who was killed on the night before Yalda Eve.

Aha! Isn't it a trivial story?

Trivial for others, but not for me. For your naïve little sis, it's a titanic question mark.

I see! So, let's go to my place.

I was at the cemetery today.

In Tehran's cemetery, Behesht-e Zahra?

No! In Mount Royal Cemetery.

Let's go! They're on the scene, waiting for us to perform their ceremonial murder.

Who are "they?"

My murderers.

But your wife and your twins killed you eighteen years ago, Dadash Yunes.

They're going to kill me once, kill me twice, kill me three times, Sis.

They multiplied the crime by three and divided the punishment into three. You've been dead for eighteen years.

I'm cordially inviting you to the murder ceremony of Yunes Negunbakht. Your Dadashi already died a long, long time ago, Little Sis—when he lost Mati.

"When Big Heart stops beating, Big Brain damage occurs." That's what you said. Not to me, though. To Turan, our neighbour's daughter.

You were too young to get it then.

And Turan got it enough to reject your proposal, saying that you loved your sisters more than her.

Your mom messed up.

She did. But you loved Mati.

And you didn't keep Mati's memento for me.

The black skirt? Ah! It was a fabulous floral gypsy skirt.

It's good that you remember that.

Of course. She got it from Ferdowsi. She put it on at once, and then we all went to Café Naderi.

It was her last summer.

Sorry, Dadashi. I couldn't have known that Maman Ashi would make a pot lid cover from a keepsake. It was in her antique chest for years. I thought she'd kept it for me—it didn't fit Sister Eti's massive rear end.

That fucking hag did it to screw me over.

Huh? Don't forget your stepmother ended up rotting inside, in her guts, and that no perfume could bring anybody back to her bed!

Come on! A shitty death, like a shitty life, doesn't prove the existence of a fair, shit-throwing god. Don't forget all the women who crushed me—from my feeble mom who kicked the bucket and left me alone at the age of two, to my rural nanny who was a carbon copy of Mme. Thénardier, to my stepmother, to my wife and my older daughter who...

Don't overlook your son, Yunes. Brainwashed or not, both your daughter and your son assisted their mom in killing you. And you, my beloved Little Sis, weren't you a traitor as well? Traitor?

Tell me! You and that snob, Piruz, didn't you look down on me and my family? He left home after you accepted custody of Iran and Turaj, and then you yielded custody of them to their ornery grandfather!

Okay. Think of me as a traitor! I felt helpless and lost in a life that was in shambles—days of taking care of my baby and your kids, nights grieving your horrible death in the company of a jinn. True, I gave up the idea of taking care of Turaj and Iran; not only because they were lying to me to support their mom, but also because I wanted to save my son and myself from hell. It's also true, though, that in addition to your denying Islam, and your blasphemous, unholy references to God, your overbearing behaviour and paranoid thoughts led to your death.

Paranoid thoughts? What do you mean?

Yes, your thoughts were as bad as poison ivy. They gave you horrible rashes—worse than those caused by food allergies. And please don't scratch yourself. You've made your skin like an elephant hide.

Fair enough. But right in the middle of heaven, everything around me makes me itchy. I'd better leave you alone and go back to the thorny bosom of my family.

Rolling over in bed, rolling in the deep, Yalda has a feeling of being pushed forward by gusts of icy wind in a narrow, dark tunnel. With her feet dangling above the ground, she feels like a bat. When she finds herself in the tunnel's mouth, she sees a dark red sunset—the sky looks like a tent with surreal hues and shades over a domestic urban landscape. Far from the frigid Montreal night, she senses the dusty twilight of downtown Tehran. She flies away, up in the sky, towards a shabby house. She knows it is going to become a crime scene. As she approaches, she spots the landmarks of her brother's house: the persimmon tree, barren of leaves but still holding some of its translucent orange orbs, and a white used Fiat 124 in the yard with the hood up. She is in the right spot. She sits on top of the wall. The prospective victim is in the middle of the veranda, sitting on his favourite white sheepskin, surrounded by basic carpentry tools. He hardly looks like her lovely Dadash Yunes. With a newly shaved balding head, a bulging belly, and face like leather, he is now known as Yunes Negunbakhat. He is supposed to get three bangs on the head, to prove his last name fits him perfectly. Although she doesn't have the same name any more, she is about to see that she is not immune to his curse. She doesn't feel like a bat, or Batwoman, anymore. Instead, she feels like a bird—a very small bird that can't flap its wings or bob its head. It is as if she turned to stone the moment she perched on the wall—unable to flutter and twitter, but still able to see. All she can do is watch. She possesses the two dot-like, moist eyes of a little bird caught within a stone head. The poor living bird, trapped within the stone *matryoshka* bird, has no choice but to become a witness to a very simple murder.

With her right eye, she sees Yunes, ignorant of his fate, busy making a small wooden doll for his favourite child, Iran. Her left eye observes the eight-year-old girl, in the kitchen, where the twins, Turan and Turaj, are gathered around their mom, Ensi. Her right eye, fixed on Yunes, sees that despite his constant scratching, he is absorbed in his woodwork. When Turaj and Iran pass him quietly to go to the yard, he turns his head. Pointing to the piece of wood in his hand, he addresses Iran with a hint of a smile. "Look, Iran! It's going to be yours!" The girl, lingering for a minute, looks over her shoulder and says, "It's not going to be a Barbie, Dad." As the girl disappears behind the car, the pale smile on his face is replaced with a lopsided one. Muttering a curse, he wrinkles his brow and resumes shaping the wood in his rough hands.

Behind the car, Turaj, holding Iran's hand, leads her toward the toilet next to the shed in the corner of the yard. They go inside, and after a few minutes Turaj comes out and closes the door, hidden from his father's sight by the car with the popped hood. He goes back to the house, making a detour to avoid passing Yunes. Yalda's left eye can see him back in the kitchen, nodding and staring into his mom's cold blue eyes. His eyes, although brown like Yunes's, are not expressive like his. While his other facial features resemble his father's, their combination makes him look completely different. His twin sister is the opposite: although her eyes are the same blue as her mother's, Yalda can see that she looks disturbed while Ensi is calm and collected. Turan, standing beside the bubbling *samovar* on the countertop, blinks and opens and closes her mouth a few times like a fish. The right eye observes Yunes looking down at his almost empty glass of tea. He dunks a sugar cube and then tosses it into his mouth, sucking noisily. To disregard her brother's disgusting habit, she returns her focus to the other eye. Now, Ensi has a wooden stick like a baton in her hands. It is one among dozens of unwanted items that Yunes has found on the street and collected—he has pack rat tendencies. While Ensi and Turaj look composed, Turan is blinking her eyes and wrinkling her nose. Yunes's shout fills the kitchen: "Where the hell are you, Ensi? Can't you bring me another glass of hot tea?"

"I'll bring it in a minute," Ensi replies, loudly but calmly. Without exchanging looks with the twins, she steps forward. They follow her. All of a sudden, the poor bird's heart begins beating quickly, and its left eye goes blind, as if it was struck with a dart. The right eye, sharper than before, zooms in onto the veranda. Now Ensi is behind Yunes, who is cutting a mortise to make an eye for the doll. Like an eagle bent on its prey, with his upper body bent forward, he is completely focused on his job. When Ensi lifts up the wooden stick solemnly, Yunes flinches, as if he feels somebody behind him. The stone head keeps its mouth shut, and the caged bird feels a ball of fire in its throat. When the stick hits Yunes's bare head, Ensi, ritualistic and with a steely tone, utters, "We kill you once." Her voice grates on the bird's nerves. The chisel falls out of Yunes's right hand, but he grabs his club hammer, which is beside him. He turns to look behind him. In disbelief, his eyes pass over Ensi and settle on Turan and Turaj. He loses his grip on the hammer and tips his head to one side. The stick, this time in Turan's hand, hits his head. "We kill you twice," says Ensi in the same manner and with the same tone. "Thank you all," Yunes murmurs, trying to turn back. He fails, and a crooked smile appears on his deformed face. The tiny bird, suddenly beating its wings, can see the blood seeping out of his head wound. While Yunes lifts his arm to wipe the blood from his eyes, Turaj grabs the stick to deliver the third blow to his head. "We kill you three times." The final repetition of the murderous refrain, performed by Ensi, declares that the job is done. Now, the right eye sees the man, who happened to be called Yunes Negunbakhat, collapse slowly on his white sheepskin rug and remain in the fetal position.

And then the darkness falls upon her. Again, she hears the echo: Bang! Bang! Bang!

Mais non, *my jinn, don't stare at me with your pathetic puppy face. Let me go! Don't mistake me for Yalda! I'm just a shadow—one among thirty or thirty in one. Whatever, it's time to depart, time to be done, time to take the road of no return. All I want is to go and not look back. Leave me alone and do whatever you want: turn into smoke and find a crack to go out of, or creep into the pile of woodles and merge with them. Be a nice jinn and disappear from my sight! I'm not going to stay in this cage. I'm not going to bear the solid body of a stone bird. I'm not going to swallow the fire ball in my throat. I will wake from this hellish nightmare and stop whimpering about what I've left behind. See? I'm detached from everything, every tie to the past. I'm opening my eyes to my solitude. A cell will not confine me anymore.*

It is a blackout of light and mind. The face of the deep is dark. From somewhere unknown, a dream appears. The fire, blazing inside, lets a cave take shape in front of invisible, searching eyes. The cave has no mouth open towards the light; yet it holds a fire-lit wall that looks like a white screen. Instead of shadows of chained prisoners, it displays a familiar setting: the shadow man's studio in the dark hour before dawn. A body, lying down on the bed, looks dead under the reddish light. There is no trace of either the jinn or the puppeteer. The white canvas curtain, pulled halfway up, marks the line between two distinct realms: the stillness of the body at rest, and the stirring motion of the thirty birds that circle around the altar. The stack of woodles, organized and placed on the altar, is stable under the pressure of the small club hammer. The commotion comes from the chattering of the weird little birds with human faces. While their bodies are almost the same, their faces express different emotions. As the longest night loses its battle with a breaking dawn, their features become more evident. The first glow of a cold aurora touches the eyelids of the body, waking her up. She sees a patch of sunlight that heralds the new day on the shady wall before her. It's time to get ready for departure. On the doorstep, with her hand on the knob, she lingers, taking a quick look back. Among the birds, Yalda's face catches her eye. When she opens the door to leave the cell, she hears a familiar echo in her head:

AND IT WAS NOT A DREAM!

Acknowledgements

It took me long, hard years to write this novel. I would like to express my gratitude to the Writers' Trust of Canada for providing assistance that allowed me the opportunity to finally finish it. I would also like to thank Luciana Ricciutelli, the editor-in-chief of Inanna Publications, and all involved in publishing the book. And last but not least, my thanks to Attar, the great Persian poet and sufi, who wrote *The Canticle of the Birds*; to Plato, who led me to his "Cave"; and to all real and imaginary shadows, who never leave me alone.

Photo: Hoda Ghods

Born in Tehran in 1953, Fereshteh Molavi lived and worked there until 1998 when she immigrated to Canada. She worked and taught at Yale University, University of Toronto, York University, and Seneca College. She was a fellow at Massey College and a writer-in-residence at George Brown College. Molavi has published many works of fiction and non-fiction in Persian in Iran and Europe. She has been the recipient of awards for novesl and translation. Her first book in English, *Stories from Tehran,* was released in 2018. She lives in Toronto.